When I Grow Up...Just Imagine.

ISBN 978-1-721-12987-4

Made in the USA

This book is dedicated to my beautiful children ~ Madison Michelle Oliver and Brendan David Oliver. My inspirations! May you find what you love to do, and go for it!

Dear Reader:

I am not an expert. I am writing from my own experiences and from the heart. I want you to find your passion and follow your dreams. Just imagine...

~ Erica Brown Oliver

Table of Contents

Introduction ... Pages 7

Thought Bubble Tips ... Pages 9-37

My Profile ... Page 39
What do you like to do?

Industries and Professions ... Pages 40-221
Including the following industries and professions:

Accounting	Music
Advertising	Non-Profit
Arts	Operations Management
Banking	Performing Arts
Business Development	Politics
Civil Service	Project Management
Education	Real Estate
Engineering	Religion
Entertainment	Retail
Entrepreneurship	Sales
Finance	Science
Graphic Design	Social Service
Healthcare	Social Work
Human Resources	Spirituality
Law	Sports
Law Enforcement	Sports Management
Manufacturing	Technology
Marketing	Travel
Media	Wholesale Management
Motivational Speaking	Yoga

Word Search ... Page 223

My Connections ... Pages 225-245
Conduct your own interviews using the blank templates provided.

List of Industries and Professions ... Pages 247-251

Letters to Parents/Guardians ... Pages 255-257

Conclusion ... Pages 259

Introduction

Great news! There are so many things that you can be when you grow up. Don't worry about it now. Just flip through the pages and see a glimpse of some of the many professions that are out there.

The awesome people featured in this book were once in elementary and middle school too! When they were your age, most of them did not know exactly what they wanted to be when they grew up. But they had great imaginations, just like you! In many cases, seeing people in various professions as they grew older, plus exposure to many different occupations, led them to the careers that they have now. You will see the college(s) each person attended and/or training they have had, what they studied, and what led them on their career path. And, guess what? Each person featured is continually learning and growing in their profession, and some have more than one!

So...take your time and go through this book. Keep it as a reference. Ask your parents if you have questions. They love to answer questions!

Please note: The descriptions and fun and interesting thoughts shared by the featured professionals are a reflection of their own experiences.

Thought Bubble Tips

Thought Bubble Tips

Check out the 14 **thought bubble** tips on the following pages. These tips may help you figure out what you want to be when you grow up. They are things for you to think about while imagining the possibilities. You will find suggestions on how to use your **imagination**, find your **passion**, **visualize** your future and set **goals**. There are also tips encouraging you to **read**, **lead**, get great **grades**, **practice** and stay **motivated**. As you get older, and you find professions that you are interested in, you can learn more about them by **shadowing**, **volunteering**, having a **mentor** and a **network**. Most of all, you should be **happy** and enjoy life every day!

Read through the **thought bubble** tips. They are ideas for you to consider and keep in mind. And you know what? You are already doing many of them!

#1
Imagine

Thought Bubble Tip

#1
Imagine

Use your imagination to think of the many things that you can be when you grow up. Did you know that you are already being exposed to the effects of many professions daily? When you go to the store, when you are watching TV, and even when you are looking out the window of a car, you are seeing the work of many different professions.

When you are at the grocery store, imagine how the products got on the shelves. Many products went through several people like Farmers, Manufacturers, Distributers, Advertisers and more, before arriving to the store. When you watch TV, think about who worked on the show that you are watching; Writers, Producers, Directors, Editors, Location Managers, Camera Operators, Agents, Actors and more! When you are riding past traffic lights, buildings, highways and bridges, imagine how they got there. There are many professions that participated in getting those structures constructed; Architects, Engineers, Contractors, Construction Workers, Project Managers and many more!

Think about all of the things you can be! Just imagine...

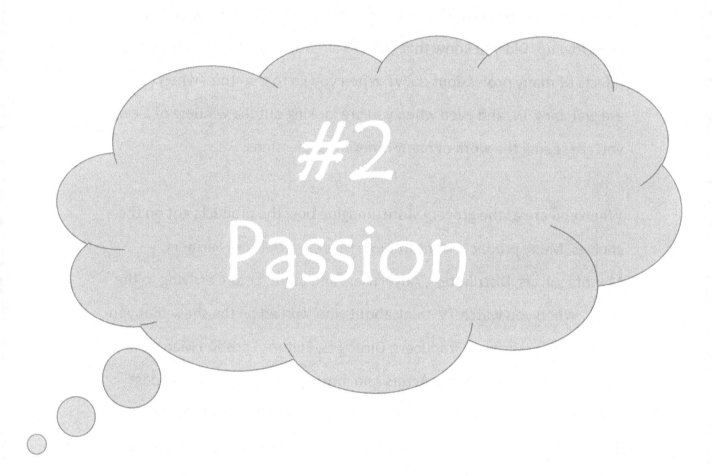

#2
Passion

Thought Bubble Tip

#2
Passion

Think about your passions. The things you are so excited to do and can't wait to do in your spare time, are the things that you are passionate about. If you know what you are passionate about, and you pursue it, it could become your profession. And, wouldn't it be nice to go to work every day doing the thing you truly love to do?

Just imagine... What do you love to do? Do you have a hobby? Do you like creating things with your hands? Do you like writing? Do you like solving mysteries? Do you like music? Do you enjoy math? Puzzles? Science? Do you like watching sports? Playing sports? Do you enjoy building things? Do you enjoy helping others?

If you do not know what you're **passionate** about right now, it is okay. You may not have been exposed to it yet. Do not worry. There's plenty of time. But when you notice things that you are really good at, or when you have an eagerness to do certain things, projects, assignments or tasks, maybe that's it!

14

Thought Bubble Tip

Visualize the things that you love to do. Make a vision board representing you and the things you enjoy. It's easy to create. Look through magazines and cut out pictures and words that are related to the things that you like. Glue them to a poster board, and put it in a place where you will see it every day.

If you already know what you would like to be when you grow up, visualize it! Try to see yourself in that profession. If you want to be a Surgeon, picture yourself as a Surgeon speaking with your patients. If you want to be a Civil Engineer imagine yourself as a Civil Engineer standing in front of a building that you helped create. If you want to be a Writer, picture yourself as a Writer with published books, produced TV shows, Broadway plays or whatever your writing goals may be. If you want to have your own business, invent apps, make music, or, be an Animator, Video Game Creator, Chef, Chemist, Curator, Designer, Judge, Professor, Meteorologist, Neuroscientist, Philanthropist ... anything you want to be, **visualize** yourself in that profession.

If you can see it, you are taking a huge step towards making it come true!

#4
Goals

Thought Bubble Tip

#4
Goals

Did you know that you already set goals for yourself? Yes, you do. Have you ever said to yourself…"I'm going to get an A on my spelling test tomorrow", or "I'm going to try and score 8 points in my game today", or "I'm going to read for a half hour tonight"? When you set your mind to do something and you are determined to do it, you are setting a goal.

Start a journal and write down your thoughts and ideas. You can set short-term and long-term goals. It is good to give yourself goals because it is a way to help you strive. Plus, it feels good to reach a **goal**.

You can set goals for the things that you are passionate about. A goal could be to learn more about your passion, to practice every day, or to move up to the next level. Once you reach a goal, enjoy the moment, check it off of your list and set more!

Thought Bubble Tip

A good way to learn more about any subject is to read. Reading expands your knowledge and allows you to use your imagination. You should read for at least a half hour every day.

Look for books in the genres (categories) that interest you. Do you like mysteries, comedies, biographies or graphic novels? Look for books on topics that grab your attention. Are you interested in airplanes, animals, plants, travel, human rights, other countries or planets? If so, read books on those subjects.

Read all that you can regarding your passion. You can **read** books, magazines, newspapers and articles online. The more information you have about it, the more you will be able to understand it. If you really like tennis... practice, watch videos, learn from those who are already professional and read tennis books. If you love fashion... research your favorite designer and read books on the history of fashion. If you are interested in science, technology, engineering, arts and mathematics, read books on STEAM. Whatever you are interested in, read, read and read more about it.

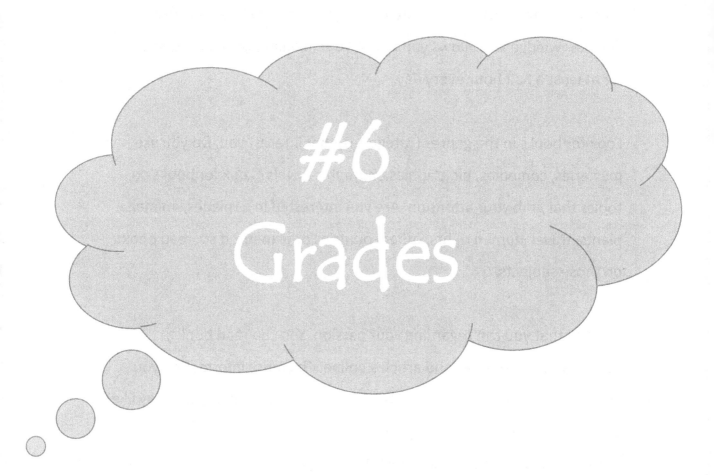

Thought Bubble Tip

#6
Grades

Try your hardest to get great grades. Strive for the A+ and the ✓+. Your education is so important. Be a good listener and learn all that you can about each subject.

If you are having a little difficulty with a subject, ask for help. If you do not understand something your teacher is reviewing, ask questions. If you need help, do not be afraid to ask. You may be able to get extra help during school, after school or arrange to have a tutor. It is better to make sure that you understand right away, so that you do not fall behind.

Give every assignment your all and do your best. Also, review your work and make sure that you are proud of everything that you do.

Getting good **grades** will lead to more opportunities!

#7
Practice

Thought Bubble Tip

#7
Practice

In order to get better at anything, you must practice. Try and try again. Do it over and over. How did you learn your ABCs? You practiced. If you play a team sport, you will always have practice. You **practice** to get better.

Mistakes may happen along the way, and it's okay, as long as you learn from them. If you make mistakes, try not to get frustrated and DO NOT GIVE UP. You can do it!

I am sure that you have heard the phrase "practice makes perfect". If it is something that you really enjoy…. practice, practice, practice. In your spare time, continue to practice. Set goals and see how much you improve. You will get even better than you imagined!

#8
Encourage

Thought Bubble Tip

Have you ever clapped for anyone? Have you ever said to someone "Good game"? If so, then you are encouraging that person. It is good to show people that they are doing a great job. And, it is nice for you to hear it as well. It's a great feeling!

You can also **encourage** yourself by telling yourself you are doing a great job. If you ever get discouraged, don't get down on yourself. Stay focused, positive and confident. You are great! You are awesome! And, you can do it!

Saying encouraging things makes a person feel good. Look in the mirror and tell yourself that you can accomplish your goals. And, you will.

Encourage

#9
Lead

Thought Bubble Tip

You are a leader! You already lead. Have you ever helped a classmate with an assignment? Have you every shown a friend how to solve a problem? Have you ever helped a friend when they got hurt? Have you ever stepped up to be a team captain? Have you ever been on student council? Have you ever helped guide your younger sibling? Whenever you take the **lead**, you are a leader.

A good leader works well within a **team**, listens and encourages everyone to share their ideas, and makes unified decisions (bringing everything together).

Continue to be a leader. Encourage yourself to step up. Don't be afraid to volunteer to take the lead. You can do it!

#10
Mentor

Thought Bubble Tip

#10
Mentor

A person who wants to share their knowledge of their profession can be a mentor. A person who is willing to share their expertise can be a mentor. A good mentor will give you information on specific areas of interest and guide you in the right direction.

Once you know what you are passionate about, a person who has experience in that area can help you.

Your parent may be able to find a mentor for you. It may be a family member or a trusted friend. A good **mentor** will be able to share information, answer questions, and suggest steps for you to take to pursue your passion.

#11
Shadow

Thought Bubble Tip

#11
Shadow

A good way to tell if you really want to be in a certain profession is to shadow a person in that profession. By shadowing, you are following the person around on their job. Listening, watching and observing them during their daily work routine.

If your parents know someone in the profession that you are interested in, they may be able to arrange a time for you to meet with that person and/or possibly go to work with them for a few hours one day. Summer is a great time of year to do this.

Ask the person that you are shadowing lots of questions. **Shadowing** will allow you to get a better understanding of the profession and it will give you the opportunity to see if you really like it.

#12
Volunteer

Thought Bubble Tip

#12
Volunteer

When you volunteer, you are helping. Volunteering is a great way to learn more about a profession.

If there is something that you are interested in, try to **volunteer**. If you love animals, see if you can volunteer at your local pet hospital or veterinarian office. If you enjoy talking about sports, volunteer to report on your town's youth sporting events. If you like helping others, ask if there are any local community service opportunities.

Use your imagination. Whatever you are interested in, there may be a way to volunteer.

#13
Network

Thought Bubble Tip

#13
Network

Right now, your networks are your friends, family and any team, club or organization you are in. A network usually consist of people with similar interest.

You will hear the words 'network' and 'networking', more and more as you get older. When you are **networking**, you are meeting people and sharing information regarding things you are interested in.

When you start to become more focused on, or more interested in certain subjects or clubs or sports, your network will get larger. You will meet more people who like the same things, learn more about those things and your friendships will grow too!

#14
Happy

Thought Bubble Tip

Most of all...be **happy**!!! Enjoy your life!

Don't be afraid to try new things. Have fun!

Smile, laugh, play! Explore, wonder...

My Profile

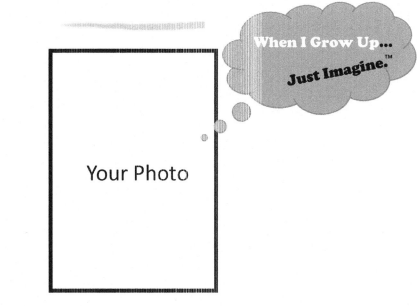

When I Grow Up...
Just Imagine.™

Name: _____

1. What are your hobbies?
   _____

   _____

2. What do you like to do for fun?
   _____

   _____

3. When you have free time, what do you like to do?
   _____

   _____

4. What are your favorite subjects in school?
   _____

   _____

5. What are you interested in learning more about?
   _____

   _____

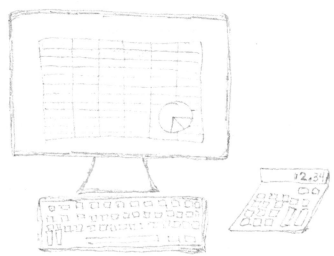

"I've always enjoyed working with numbers and accounting allows me to do this every day."

~ Lindsey Desiderio

Accounting

Lindsey Desiderio
Senior Accountant

College/University: **Quinnipiac University** (Hamden, CT)
Major: **Accounting**

Description of your profession:
I help make sure my company's financial records are kept accurately throughout the year. Which means that I keep track of all of the money coming into the company and going out of the company.

Why did you choose this profession?
I've always enjoyed working with numbers, and accounting allows me to do this every day.

What is interesting about your profession?
It's like a large puzzle that you need to put together to make sure everything balances correctly.

What do you like most about your profession?
1. Working in special computer programs for finance and setting up spreadsheets.
2. Being able to do some sort of math every day.
3. Interacting with other departments within the company to help them set financial goals throughout the year.

"I chose this profession because I have a way with words and I enjoy using them to get the attention of an audience."

~ Dan Gabbay

Advertising

Dan Gabbay
Writer

College/University: **Boston University** (Boston, MA)
Major: **English Literature**

Description of your profession:
I write advertisements and marketing materials, for printed pieces, television and the internet. I also write books. When writing advertisements, I think about who the ad is trying to appeal to – the audience – and I write to reach them. My aim is to write the kind of story that will make the audience want to know more. It's the same when I write a book, just on a bigger scale. It is still storytelling, whether in a five word headline or a fifty thousand word book. I often do research on the internet to find helpful information to write those stories.

Why did you choose this profession?
I have a way with words and I enjoy using them to get the attention of an audience.

What is interesting about your profession?
Whether writing a tweet or a book, it's all about telling stories.

What do you like most about your profession?
1.   I get to do research and interviews, and by doing so, I learn new things.
2.   It's a fun challenge to take a lot of information and write about it in a way that excites interest.
3.   Sometimes I work on my own and sometimes with others.

"I've always been a visual person who thrived in writing and production and film making, therefore, the art of storytelling was a natural fit for me."

~ Lori Bullock

Advertising / Film Production

Lori Bullock
Vice President, Executive Integrated Producer

College/University: **St. John's University** (Jamaica, NY)
Major: **Communications Arts**

Description of your profession:
I manage and oversee the development of content production for advertisers. Content production is the process of developing and creating written or visual pieces. I get to bring ideas to life, and it ends with a finished product for the viewer to experience. That process is done in project phases, from brainstorming the story board all the way through production, to the final edit, which includes: commercials, behind the scene documentaries and branded content.

Why did you choose this profession?
I've always been a visual person who thrived in writing and production and film making, therefore, the art of storytelling was a natural fit for me.

What is interesting about your profession?
The thing about producing advertising campaigns for various products, services and technological innovators, is that it provides me the opportunity to learn a great deal about many things, in order to effectively market it to the masses (a large number of people).

What do you like most about your profession?
1. The ability to travel around the world shooting advertising campaigns.
2. Working with innovative artists, such as top caliber (quality) directors, actors and photographers.
3. Developing a piece of content for the world to see that started as a simple idea.

"I chose this profession because it has allowed me to help advance our artistic legacy to the next generation."

~ Eric Pryor

The Arts

Eric Pryor
President

College/University (undergraduate): **Wayne State University** (Detroit, MI)
Major: **Fine Arts**
College/University (graduate): **Temple University** (Philadelphia, PA)
MFA: **Master of Fine Arts – Concentration in Painting**
Other education/certification: **Non-profit Management Certificate, Columbia University** (New York, NY)

Description of your profession:
Arts administrators chart visions for the organization and deal with the business operations around an arts organization. Arts administrators are responsible for facilitating (helping along) the day-to-day operations of the organization; like supervising staff, making sure the clients and customers are happy, meeting with stakeholders like donors, community leaders and parents. And, we are responsible for fulfilling its mission (goal).

Why did you choose this profession?
It has allowed me to help advance our artistic legacy to the next generation.

What is interesting about your profession?
It's interesting to see young artists find their creative voice.

What do you like most about your profession?
1.   I am excited to see the growth in the organization.
2.   Watching the creative process unfold.
3.   Seeing children perform.

"I enjoy sharing my knowledge and developing the next generation of financial professionals."

~ Oran C. Bowry

Banking

Oran C. Bowry
Senior Vice President & Division Manager

College/University (undergraduate): **Rutgers University** (New Brunswick, NJ)
Major: **Labor Studies**
College/University (graduate): **University of the Virgin Islands** (Charlotte Amalie West, St. Thomas, USVI)
MBA: **Master of Business Administration - Concentration in Finance**

Description of your profession:
I plan and manage the bank's retail operations and credit portfolios (a range of investments held by a people or organization) within the U.S. Virgin Islands and British Virgin Islands. This includes oversight for all branches and cash processing centers, mortgage credit centers, commercial banking centers, insurance and administrative services.

Why did you choose this profession?
I began my banking career as a Human Resource Manager, but realized the operations and lending areas of banking offered me more challenges and rewards.

What is interesting about your profession?
Working with new small business entrepreneurs. I get to help develop their ideas and dreams into successful businesses.

What do you like most about your profession?
1. The public relations aspect of my job allows me to be involved in various community service initiatives. For example, the bank installed water purification systems on the island following hurricanes Irma and Maria.
2. Sharing my knowledge and developing the next generation of financial professionals.
3. Negotiating multi-million dollar credit deals.

"I've always had an interest in working with numbers and with people."

~ Darlene Winkler

Banking

Darlene Winkler
Director

College/University: **Rutgers University** (New Brunswick, NJ)
Major/Minor: **Economics/English**

Description of your profession:
I am a Relationship Executive, responsible for building global relationships and providing excellent service and support for mutual fund and insurance clients. I am also responsible for selling additional bank products to support the clients strategic plan. The bank offers a number of services and products for our clients to buy. One service requires that the bank hold or safekeep client assets. The client assets are usually in the form of cash, stocks and bonds. We make sure that we keep these items safe and provide regular accounting for the amount of cash and the positions for stocks and bonds. We can hold these types of assets in over 120 markets, including Hong Kong, Denmark, Italy and Spain.

Why did you choose this profession?
I've always had an interest in working with numbers and with people.

What is interesting about your profession?
We are a global bank and I have the opportunity to work with colleagues around the world (London, England, Dublin, Ireland and India).

What do you like most about your profession?
1. Traveling around the world to meet colleagues and clients.
2. We have a state-of-the-art office space that inspires collaboration and teamwork.
3. Having the flexibility to work from home or work in the office.

"After several years of developing my education and work experience in the areas of accounting, economics and banking practice, I gained an interest in IT (Information Technology)."

~ Stephanie Williams

Regulatory Banking

Stephanie Williams
Examination Specialist – Information Technology (IT)

College/University: **Long Island University** (Brooklyn, NY)
Major: **Finance**

Description of your profession:
I am primarily responsible for activities related to IT (Information Technology) reviews of banks and data centers in the NY area and surrounding states. IT is the use of computer hardware, software, and networks to store, transfer, and process electronic information related to a business. A data center is the location of a bank's computer and storage systems, and telecommunications parts.

Why did you choose this profession?
After several years of developing my education and work experience in the areas of accounting, economics and banking practice, I gained an interest in IT and how it relates to financial institutions and data centers.

What is interesting about your profession?
Meeting with financial institution Directors and other high-level banking officials to discuss IT security issues. Security issues are events that result in unauthorized access to a bank customer's account. This is done by bypassing security controls within the bank. An example may be ATM PIN code theft.

What do you like most about your profession?
1. Participating in conferences and learning about emerging information technologies.
2. Being able to travel to different places within the United States.
3. The work/life balance enables me to work from home when I need to.

"I decided that I wanted to pursue the rabbinate as a
career, since Judaism and Jewish practices are what
really motivated me more than anything else."

~ Rabbi Zvi Karpel

Chaplain

Rabbi Zvi Karpel
Chaplain

College/University (undergraduate): **State University of New York at Albany** (Albany, NY)
Major: **English**
College/University (graduate): **Wurzweiler School of Social Work** (New York, NY)
MSW: **Master of Social Work**
Other education/certification: **Rabbinic Ordination from Yeshiva University's Rabbinic Program – Rabbi Isaac Elchanan Theological Seminary (RIETS)** (New York, NY)

Description of your profession:
My congregation (group who gather for religious worship) consists of patients in a hospital or residents in a nursing home. This profession requires its own training known as CPE (Clinical Pastoral Education). I provide the opportunity for residents to be able to express Jewish observances.

Why did you choose this profession?
While in college I assisted in having the university create a kosher kitchen that brought together students interested in Jewish observance. Shortly afterwards, I decided that I wanted to pursue the rabbinate as a career, since Judaism and Jewish practices are what really motivated me more than anything else.

What is interesting about your profession?
I get to share my knowledge and make a difference in the Jewish community.

What do you like most about your profession?
1. Celebrating the holiday of Purim with the residents.
2. Visiting with residents, listening to their stories and uplifting their spirits.
3. I feel fulfilled when offering pastoral care to families at critical times of grave illness.

"I chose this profession because I was looking for an opportunity to simultaneously be an active participant in my community and make a positive impact on the future of society."

~ Nadia Yar

Education

Nadia Yar
Teacher

College/University (undergraduate): **Montclair State University** (Montclair, NJ)
Major: **Psychology**
College/University (graduate): **Montclair State University** (Montclair, NJ)
MAT: **Master of Arts in Teaching**
Other education/certification: **Certified Teacher K-5**

Description of your profession:
I am a Gifted and Talented teacher that teaches elementary students who perform remarkably high in subjects like Math and Language Arts. I also teach STEM (Science, Technology, Engineering and Math) to third and fourth grade students. I help my students learn how to access their creative potential and apply them to solve all kinds of real-world problems.

Why did you choose this profession?
I was looking for an opportunity to simultaneously be an active participant in my community and make a positive impact on the future of society.

What is interesting about your profession?
I get to watch the future leaders of our world become curious problem-solvers, excited to work together and share ideas.

What do you like most about your profession?
1. Meeting so many interesting people (kids and adults) who teach me so much about life.
2. Not a day goes by that I don't get to laugh with kids.
3. I get to do fun STEM projects with my students and celebrate in their achievements.

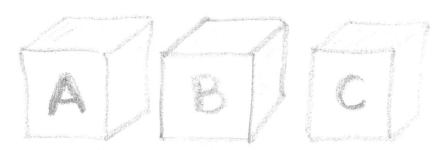

"Every day I get to help children explore, investigate, uncover and discover the world around them."

~ Maggie Magro

Education

Maggie Magro
Preschool Teacher

College/University (undergraduate): **Seton Hall University** (South Orange, NJ)
Major/Minor: **Business/Marketing**
College/University (graduate): **Montclair State University** (Montclair, NJ)
Other education/certification: **Alternate Route program for Teaching: Early Childhood Education**

Description of your profession:
I started my career in the business world and also worked in the children's entertainment industry. I realized my passion for children and decided to change careers when the business world changed after 9-11-2001. (My train pulled into the station at World Trade when the first plane hit).

Why did you choose this profession?
To make a difference in the lives of children by helping them become good human beings so that they can make the world a better place for the future.

What is interesting about your profession?
Every day, I get to help children explore, investigate, uncover and discover the world around them; filling their minds with curiosity, their hearts with love of learning and their lives with knowledge.

What do you like most about your profession?
1. Each day, presents opportunities to explore new topics and share experiences.
2. Children experience the excitement of learning through play and interaction.
3. There is an indescribable feeling of fulfillment that I get from seeing those tiny, smiling faces every day.

"I chose teaching because I desire to equip children with skills that will help them throughout their lives."
~ Karen Richburg

Education

Karen Richburg
Educator

College/University (undergraduate): **Virginia State University** (Petersburg, VA)
Major: **Business Management**
College/University (graduate): **Hunter College** (New York, NY)
M.S.Ed.: **Master of Science in Education - Concentration in Elementary Education**

Description of your profession:
I educate children from Pre Kindergarten to 6th grade. It is my passion and joy to create an environment conducive to active learning in which children can use their gifts, talents and interests while they learn.

Why did you choose this profession?
I chose teaching because I desire to equip (prepare) children with skills that will help them throughout their lives. In addition, seeing joy on their faces when they've learned something new, is priceless!

What is interesting about your profession?
It is invaluable. The fact is, every human being would have had a teacher in some capacity in their lives.

What do you like most about your profession?
1. Infusing my gift of the arts in each subject I teach, making it enjoyable for my students.
2. Using music to teach almost any subject.
3. Working really hard, and playing just as hard. We have those awesome holidays off and long breaks!

"I get to be myself – funny, creative, positive – and help kids understand that Math can be fun and easy."

~ Stephanie Hykey

Education

Stephanie Hykey
Teacher

College/University (undergraduate): **Seton Hall University** (South Orange, NJ)
Major/Minor: **Elementary Education/Social Behavior/Psychology**
College/University (graduate): **Seton Hall University** (South Orange, NJ)
MA: **Master of Arts - Concentration in Special Education**
Other education/certification: **Certified Teacher Special Education, Elementary K-8 and P-3**

Description of your profession:
I teach all students (both special needs and general population) the subject area of Math. I have my own inclusion classes and work as an inclusion support facilitator alongside general education teachers. I also teach students on the autism spectrum.

Why did you choose this profession?
It was something I always wanted to do, so that I could one day, have the time to have my own family and still have a great career.

What is interesting about your profession?
Every day is a new and different day – it's never boring!

What do you like most about your profession?
1.   Helping to shape society and being a positive influence to our children.
2.   I get to be myself - funny, creative, positive - and help kids understand that Math can be fun and easy.
3.   The fact that I love going into work each and every day.

"Since I really enjoyed working with children and I wanted to have my own business, starting a day care became my passion."

~ Zina Floyd

Education

Zina Floyd
Partner / Owner

College/University: **Rutgers University** (New Brunswick, NJ)
Major/Minor: **Communications/Marketing**

Description of your profession:
I own a private preschool chain. As an owner, I oversee all areas of the business including the finances, the teaching staff and daily operations. My goal is to make sure each child is having an enjoyable learning experience.

Why did you choose this profession?
The preschool market is a strong, growing market. And, since I really enjoyed working with children and wanted to have my own business, starting a preschool became my passion. I also have a family history of entrepreneurship, therefore, growing up and observing family members running their own businesses, gave me the ability to see myself doing the same thing.

What is interesting about your profession?
Creating a business model and seeing it to fruition (completion). I come up with all of the ideas to develop my business and I am working hard to make it successful.

What do you like most about your profession?
1.   Working with children.
2.   Developing creative new methods of teaching.
3.   Thinking of creative ways to promote my business. Building the brand and continuing to expand the business are really important to me.

"I selected the field of education to empower the lives of children."

~ Mark Daniels

Education / Administration

Mark Daniels
Middle School Principal

College/University (undergraduate): **Rutgers University** (New Brunswick, NJ)
Major/Minor: **Journalism/Mass Media; African Studies**
College/University (graduate): **Cheyney University** (Cheyney, PA)
M.Ed.: **Master of Education - Concentration in Educational Leadership**
Other education/certification: **New Jersey Principal Certification**

Description of your profession:
I serve as the instructional leader of a middle school that serves approximately 1,000 students in grades 6 through 8.

Why did you choose this profession?
I selected the field of education to empower the lives of children.

What is interesting about your profession?
I have the opportunity to witness the development and maturation of students between the ages of 10 and 14.

What do you like most about your profession?
1. The opportunity to see students and educators engaged in the process of teaching and learning each day.
2. My job involves a significant amount of verbal and written communication (with students, teachers and parents) and problem-solving.
3. Hearing the thoughts and opinions of pre-teens and teens each day.

"I am able to make an impact in the classroom by hiring the most qualified professionals who I feel will have a positive influence on the lives of students."
~ Delvis Rodriguez

Education / Administration

Delvis Rodriguez
Director of Personnel and Evaluation

College/University (undergraduate): **Drew University** (Madison, NJ)
Major: **Political Science**
College/University (graduate): **New Jersey City University** (Jersey City, NJ)
M.Ed.: **Master of Education- Concentration in Educational Leadership**
Other education/certification: **New Jersey Principal Certification**

Description of your profession:
I am in charge of all aspects of Human Resources for a large school district. I also serve as the Affirmative Action Officer and the chief liaison between all Principals and the Superintendent on personnel matters.

Why did you choose this profession?
I started working with students when I came right out of college, and I quickly realized I wanted to remain in this profession for years to come.

What is interesting about your profession?
I am able to make an impact in the classroom by hiring the most qualified professionals who I feel will have a positive influence on the lives of students.

What do you like most about your profession?
1. Every day is different.
2. Working with and learning from really smart people around me, who also want to make a difference.
3. My office environment is like a small family. I look forward to seeing them every day.

"Growing up, I wanted to be an engineer like my dad, plus I really liked learning about electricity and magnets."

~ Jessica Wood

Engineering

Jessica Wood
Engineering Manager

College/University: **Gannon University** (Erie, PA)
Major/Minor: **Electrical Engineering/Mathematics**
Other education/certification: **First Place in 2010 MTT Alive Video Competition at
IEEE/MTTS International Microwave Symposium and Pennsylvania Space Grant Participant**

Description of your profession:
I manage a group of engineers that help make and design pressure transducers for
lots of different things, such as satellites, rockets, submarines and more!

Why did you choose this profession?
Growing up, I wanted to be an engineer like my dad, plus I really liked learning about
electricity and magnets.

What is interesting about your profession?
Since there are always new things for me to figure out and discover, every day is a
little different.

What do you like most about your profession?
1. The coolest part about my job is that something I've touched and help make,
   ends up in outer space!
2. Working with lots of very smart people who help me become smarter every day.
3. The projects I work on are helping keep our country safe, strong and
   knowledgeable.

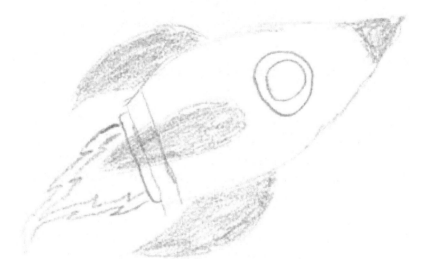

"I chose this profession because it is challenging and different every day, and making rockets and space ships is really cool!"

~ Joe Bonelli

Engineering

Joe Bonelli
Space Propulsion Materials Manager

College/University (undergraduate): **San Diego State University** (San Diego, CA)
Major: **Mechanical Engineering**
College/University (graduate): **Stephens Institute of Technology** (Hoboken, NJ)
ME: **Master of Engineering in Space Systems Engineering**
Other education/certification: **Program and Project Management Certification**

Description of your profession:
I create and design machines that make things, ranging from computer chips to toys to oil refineries, all the way to space ships and rockets.

Why did you choose this profession?
I chose this profession because it is challenging and different every day; and making rockets and space ships is really cool!

What is interesting about your profession?
Solving problems that have never been solved before, like how to go to Mars, and making things that have yet to be invented.

What do you like most about your profession?
1. Getting to see and touch things that are launched into space.
2. Working with astronauts who have actually been into space and ridden on rockets!
3. Learning new things every day from the people I work with.

"I chose this profession because I was inspired to see an industry that was being run by young black professionals shaping culture on our own terms."

~ Jameel Spencer

Entertainment

Jameel Spencer
Division President / Fashion

College/University: **Rutgers University** (New Brunswick, NJ)
Major/Minor: **Political Science/English**

Description of your profession:
I have been in the entertainment business for over 20 years helping celebrities and brands monetize their intellectual property. Meaning, I create and develop businesses by taking strengths and things the celebrities are known for, to create brands in various categories like fashion, fragrance, beauty, spirits or endorsements. I've run businesses for Shaquille O'Neal, Sean "Puffy" Combs, Shawn "Jay-Z" Carter, Pharrell Williams, Justin Timberlake and Jessica Simpson, to name a few.

Why did you choose this profession?
I chose this profession because I was inspired to see an industry that was being run by young black professionals shaping culture on our own terms.

What is interesting about your profession?
The most interesting thing about what I do is having an idea and seeing it come to fruition (realization and completion). That dynamic is exaggerated by seeing how it shapes culture.

What do you like most about your profession?
1. Traveling all over the world and spending time with some of the most interesting people of our generation.
2. I get to create.
3. I continue to learn every day from all sorts of different people.

"I wanted to see my words come to life, so I started creating short films."

~ Ericka Williams

Entertainment

Ericka Williams
Author / Teacher / Producer

College/University: **Rutgers University, Douglass College** (New Brunswick, NJ)
Major: **Communications**
Other education/certification: **New Jersey Standard Elementary School Teaching Certificate**

Description of your profession:
I produce films, fashion shows, a radio show and various events.

Why did you choose this profession?
I've always had a passion for children and making a difference in the lives of others while serving through entertainment. I was a Language Arts teacher while writing 6 novels. Having authored books and having the vision to see my dreams visually, is what led me to film production. I wanted to see my words come to life, so I started creating short films. I am looking forward to going back to college for film production, however, until then I will continue to work in areas of entertainment and media to gain more experience and learn from others.

What is interesting about your profession?
Producing shows are fun and exciting; and writing books are too!

What do you like most about your profession?
1.   Creating projects where people are able to use their imagination, enjoy and momentarily escape reality.
2.   Touching on important issues to help change the world, one project at a time.
3.   Working with other creative people who are not afraid to follow their dreams.

"I enjoy seeing the final production and knowing that I had an important role in it."

~ David Whitley

Entertainment

David Whitley
Dolly Grip

College/University: **Wheaton College** (Norton, MA)
Major/Minor: **US History/African Studies and Sociology**

Description of your profession:
I am a Grip Technician and a Dolly Grip for the film and television industry based in New York City. I've been working in film for almost 10 years in various crafts; as a Grip Technician for most of those years, and more recently as a Dolly Grip. The primary role of a Grip Technician is to cut, shape and diffuse light using various tools. As a Dolly Grip, I work side-by-side with the camera department in lining up shots for the DP (Director of Photography) and Director.

Why did you choose this profession?
I started as a production assistant and worked for two years in that position until I figured out that a Grip Technician is what I wanted to be.

What is interesting about your profession?
I help build sets, such as police stations, caves and even mansions! I rig lights to the ceiling and set the lighting mood for movies. It is a Grip Technicians job to keep everyone working on the production safe.

What do you like most about your profession?
1. Seeing the final production and knowing that I had an important role in it.
2. Building cool sets.
3. The people I work with become like my family.

"I moved to New York City and surrounded myself with creative and talented musicians and filmmakers who recognized my passion and gave me opportunities to pursue my goals."

~ Marcus Bleeker

Entertainment

Marcus Bleeker
Writer / Director / Director of Photography / Musician

College/University: **University of Wisconsin** (Madison, WI)
Major: **Music**

Description of your profession:

I am a writer, a director of small films and also a musician. As a Director of Photography; I get to establish the visual look and call the shots for the videos and films produced. As a musician, I am passionate about the drums/percussions, and I write songs for artists.

Why did you choose this profession?

I love music and I love the movies. I got started in music and film when I moved to New York City and surrounded myself with creative and talented musicians and filmmakers who recognized my passion and gave me opportunities to pursue my goals.

What is interesting about your profession?

Meeting and working with fun, creative people. I recently worked with one of the songwriters of a Broadway blockbuster musical, traveled to a world-renowned international film festival, and performed with Grammy Award winning artist Vernon Reid.

What do you like most about your profession?

1. Writing and creating interesting characters.
2. Performing for people and giving them a fun, amazing experience.
3. Traveling.

"While growing up, there were only a handful of people of color on TV, and I wanted to be a part of that change."

~ Elaine Meryl Brown

Ententainment

Elaine Meryl Brown
**Former Vice President, Creative Service, Special Markets
and Best-Selling Author**

College/University: **Wheaton College** (Norton, MA)
Major/Minor: **English/Drama**
Other education/certification: **Digital Media Marketing Mini MBA - Rutgers University** (New Brunswick, NJ) **,CTAM Executive Management Program - Harvard University School of Business** (Boston, MA) **,UCLA Anderson School of Management** (Los Angeles, CA)

Description of your profession:
As an Executive Producer, I produced TV tune-in promotion, movie trailers, branded entertainment, public service announcements, fundraising and informational tapes, as well as, original content on-and-off the network to promote the networks products and brand. As part of my job, I also lead creative teams.

Why did you choose this profession?
While growing up, there were only a handful of people of color on TV, and I wanted to be a part of that change.

What is interesting about your profession?
I get to create and have fun doing it, and at the same time, help the company attract customers and build brand loyalty.

What do you like most about your profession?
1. Generating new ideas and strategies that entertain and support business goals and objectives.
2. Working with fun, creative people and leading creative teams.
3. Building client relationships and strategic partnerships.

"As a child, I was effortlessly drawn to music as a way to expess myself."

~ Gordon Chambers

Entertainment

Gordon Chambers

Recording Artist / Songwriter / Producer / Vocal Coach / Public Speaker & Former Entertainment Editor

College/University: **Brown University** (Providence, RI)
Major/Minor: **American Studies/Journalism**

Description of your profession:
Whether on or off stage, I am involved with sharing classic timeless music – whether for myself as an artist, or other artists I have coached, mentored or written for. My discography (catalog of music) includes award winning songs for Anita Baker, Usher, Beyoncé, Aretha Franklin, Brandy, Chaka Khan, Angie Stone, Tory Lanez and more.

Why did you choose this profession?
I didn't choose music as a profession. It chose me. As a child, I was effortlessly drawn to music as a way to express myself. Sports were not for me. I was clumsy and not a "team" player. I loved the solitary confinement of practicing and creating music. I began writing and networking because I wanted my songs to be heard. It took 15 years of writing (since the age of 7), until my first placement with Queen Latifah, for a song I wrote. But the wait was worth it.

What is interesting about your profession?
Music is the soundtrack of our lives. We use and choose songs for christenings, graduations, weddings and funerals. I'm proud that songs I have written have become anthems for the chapters of the greatest emotional moments of millions of lives.

What do you like most about your profession?
1. Interacting with people, and using music to give them joy and strength.
2. I love the many facets I can work into music.
3. I am not on a fixed schedule, and every day is different.

"I love the combination of helping artists achieve
their goals and working in the entertainment
industry."

~ Ingrid French

Entertainment

Ingrid French
Talent Manager

College/University: **University of North Carolina at Chapel Hill** (Chapel Hill, NC)
Major/Minor: **Journalism and Mass Communications/Theater**

Description of your profession:
I represent actors and models for television, film, theater, commercial, voice over and print work. I advise my actors on their careers, materials and auditions, and present them to casting directors, directors, producers, agencies and photographers. These industry professionals ultimately hire them for the projects they are working on.

Why did you choose this profession?
I graduated with a degree in journalism, came to New York, and in need of immediate work, responded to a job posting for an assistant at an agency. I got the job and thought it would be temporary, however, by the end of my first day, I knew I had found my calling. I love the combination of helping artists achieve their goals and working in the entertainment industry.

What is interesting about your profession?
No two days are exactly alike and there are always new projects coming across my desk.

What do you like most about your profession?
1. Watching TV, movies and theatre as part of my job.
2. Traveling to fun and exciting places.
3. Seeing new television, film and theater projects behind the scenes, from start to finish.

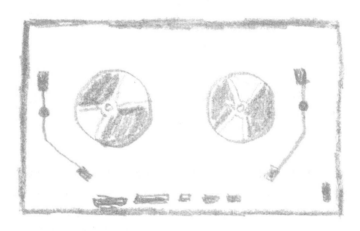

"I have a good heart and a positive mind and I get to share my energy when I play music."

~ Marvin Coleman

Entertainment

Marvin Coleman
Creative / DJ (Clubs, Events, Radio) / Music Consultant

College/University (undergraduate): **Emory University** (Atlanta, GA)
Major/Minor: **Music/Religion**
College/University (graduate): **Columbia University** (New York, NY)
MS: **Master of Science - Concentration in Journalism**

Description of your profession:
I play music to people all over the world, for their listening and/or dancing enjoyment. I put together playlists or special "mixtapes" for international entertainment companies.

Why did you choose this profession?
I like how people express themselves when they dance and feel happy because of music.

What is interesting about your profession?
Music is a universal language, and I have had the opportunity to travel and work with people from all over America and the world, including Moscow, Russia ~ Oslo, Norway ~ London, England ~ Paris, France ~ Barcelona, Spain ~ Dubai, UAE ~ Dublin, Ireland ~ Nassau, Bahamas and Acapulco, Mexico.

What do you like most about your profession?
1. I love music and music has no limits. I have fun discovering more than I know.
2. Every time I go to work, I am part of a celebration.
3. I have a good heart and a positive mind and I get to share my energy when I play music.

"I like working with numbers and analyzing trends to identify the cost associated with products or services."

~ Stacey Brown

Finance

Stacey Brown
Senior Manager, Business Analysis

College/University: **Johnson & Wales University** (Providence, RI)
Major/Minor: **Accounting/Financial Services Management**

Description of your profession:
I work in the Finance Department of an international manufacturing company. I help Marketing and Sales Managers create and track their annual budgets, and I work with department heads to develop and implement (apply) policies and procedures.

Why did you choose this profession?
I enjoy working with numbers and analyzing trends (comparing data over time) to identify the cost associated with products or services. And, I like figuring out what may cause the price of these products or services to increase or decrease.

What is interesting about your profession?
There are always new and exciting projects which make every day different.

What do you like most about your profession?
1. Traveling to different states to visit the manufacturing plants that produce our products.
2. Tasting food samples that include our products.
3. Watching how our products are produced on the manufacturing line.

"I had a passion for numbers from a very young age."

~ David Dooley

Finance

David Dooley
Vice President of Treasury Operations

College/University: **Bentley University** (Waltham, MA)
Major: **Finance**

Description of your profession:
I work with hedge funds. We value the fund's positions and then track the sum on a daily basis. This let's you know if it's a worthy investment.

Why did you choose this profession?
I had a passion for numbers from a very young age.

What is interesting about your profession?
We have a fiduciary duty (which is the highest standard of care, to act in the best interest) for our investors.

What do you like most about your profession?
1. I enjoy the people interaction.
2. The numbers.
3. The satisfaction of solving problems.

"I chose this profession because I enjoy helping others."

~ Patrick Frasier

Fire Fighter

Patrick Frasier
Fire Fighter

College/University: **East Stroudsburg University** (East Stroudsburg, PA)
Major: **Business Management**
Other education/certification: **First Aid Certification and various Fire Fighter Certifications**

Description of your profession:
As a Fire Fighter, I am a community helper. I help save peoples lives and their homes.

Why did you choose this profession?
I chose this profession because I enjoy helping others. I work in the community where I went to school and I know some of the people that we get to help; and that feels amazing! Helping people within my own community is a part of why I signed up to be a Fire Fighter.

What is interesting about your profession?
I enjoy the bond that I have with my co-workers. I help train the new fire fighters on the trucks and engines. And, I get to ride and drive the fire engine!

What do you like most about your profession?
1. Training and learning new techniques. Learning new things to protect my community and to keep me safe, is always fun!
2. Seeing the children's faces when they see or hear the fire trucks.
3. The feeling I have for my fire family is second only to my home family. The crew that I work with are my brothers. I have so much fun working with them!

"From the time I was a little boy, I've always had a passion for drawing and being creative."

~ Lou Simeone

Graphic Design

Lou Simeone
Visual Designer and Illustrator

College/University: **William Paterson University** (Wayne, NJ)
Major: **BFA (Bachelor of Fine Arts)** with a concentration in Graphic Design

Description of your profession:
Designers and Illustrators apply their artistic and creative skills to create advertising campaigns, build websites, produce logos, animations, brochures, t-shirts, sales and reference materials, and numerous other forms of visual communication. These materials are used to solve a problem, educate, communicate a message, build a brand, promote a business, a product, a cause or an event.

Why did you choose this profession?
From the time I was a little boy, I've always had a passion for drawing and being creative.

What is interesting about your profession?
My clients' industries and professions are so diverse that I could be illustrating a chicken logo for a restaurant one day and designing an eye doctor's website another.

What do you like most about your profession?
1. It's always a thrill to see my designs and illustrations out in the real world. My work has made appearances on t-shirts, skateboards, posters, work vans, logo signage for businesses, on magazine covers, in books and many other places.
2. It's great when someone who hires me, gives me the freedom to be as creative as I want.
3. It's always an honor and a pleasure when someone thinks highly of my work.

"I wanted to have a successful career where I would be able to use my creativity."

~ Cortney Provini Cole

Graphic Design

Cortney Provini Cole
Lead Designer

College/University: **University of Massachusetts -- Dartmouth** (North Dartmouth, MA)
Major: **BFA (Bachelor of Fine Arts) in Graphic Design and Typography**

Description of your profession:
I am the head Graphic Designer within the Marketing Department for wine and spirits brands. I design labels and new packaging, ad campaigns, in-store point of sale collateral (like posters, signage displays or promotional pieces), print materials, digital advertisements, and more!

Why did you choose this profession?
I wanted to have a successful career where I would be able to use my creativity.

What is interesting about your profession?
The most interesting thing about my profession is the amount of research that goes into marketing and therefore it goes into design work.

What do you like most about your profession?
1. Being able to develop new packaging solutions. This requires not only label design, but glass bottle engineering as well, which is quite challenging and interesting. I get to be creative every day which is fun!
2. Seeing my work in stores and on the shelf.
3. Being the head of the creative team. Leading, managing and guiding a team, is a different type of challenge, however, it is rewarding to watch everyone grow and be successful.

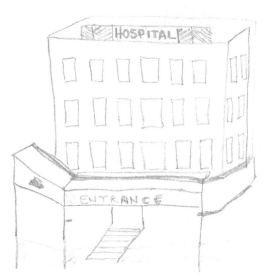

"Healthcare is a meaningful and important issue that all people will deal with at some point in their lives. I enjoy helping people."

~ Wren Mosee Lester

Healthcare / Administration

Wren Mosee Lester
Associate Vice President of Patient Experience

College/University (undergraduate): **Rutgers University** (New Brunswick, NJ)
Major: **Healthcare Administration**
College/University (graduate): **The New School NYC** (New York, NY)
MBA: **Master of Business Administration - Concentration in Health Care Administration**
College/University (doctorate): **Seton Hall University** (South Orange, NJ)
PhD: **Doctor of Philosophy (currently enrolled) - Health Care Policy and Leadership**

Description of your profession:
I make sure the hospital or health center is a good place for all of the patients. I look at how we can do things better; like giving out medications, deciding what kind of care each person will need and making sure the hospital/health center follows all the rules. My department collects information on how well each patient's surgery went, how long it takes them to get better and much more. We take this information and look for patterns and trends to help us with future patients. Most important, I work on patients getting better!

Why did you choose this profession?
Healthcare is a meaningful and important issue that all people will deal with at some point in their lives. I enjoy helping people.

What is interesting about your profession?
Quality improvement is the wave of the future and crosses all industries.

What do you like most about your profession?
1. Interacting with every department in the organization.
2. Teaching and learning new things all the time.
3. Getting to see patients bustling in and out of the lobby every day.

"From the time I was a young boy, I liked to be with older people, so I wanted to work in a place where I could help them."

~ Ken Bitman

Healthcare / Administration

Ken Bittman
Administrator

College/University (undergraduate): **State University of NY at Stony Brook** (Stony Brook, NY)
Major: **Psychology**
College/University (graduate): **Adelphi University** (Garden City, NY)
MBA: **Master of Business Administration - Concentration in Corporate Finance**
Other education/certification: **Licensed Nursing Home Administrator (LNHA)**

Description of your profession:
I am an Administrator in a skilled nursing facility. My job allows me to lead a team of caring people who help elderly people by creating a healthy place for them to live and by treating them with respect and dignity.

Why did you choose this profession?
From the time I was a young boy, I liked to be with older people, so I wanted to work in a place where I could help them.

What is interesting about your profession?
It is a wonderful challenge to lead a large group of people who each have different gifts toward a goal of helping others.

What do you like most about your profession?
1. Hearing older people tell stories about their lives.
2. Planning parties and special events that people will enjoy.
3. Meeting people from all around the world and learning about their cultures.

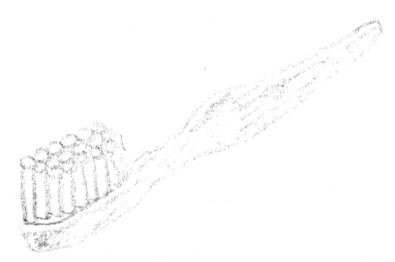

"During my 5 years of braces, I realized that I wanted to help people and work with my hands."

~ Kevin Persily, D.D.S.

Healthcare / Dental

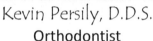

Kevin Persily, D.D.S.
Orthodontist

College/University (undergraduate): **Brooklyn College CUNY** (Brooklyn, NY)
Major/Minor: **Psychology/Biology**
Dental School: **New York University - College of Dentistry** (New York NY)
Other education/certification: **University of Medicine and Dentistry of New Jersey (UMDNJ) – School of Orthodontics** (Newark, NJ)

Description of your profession:
Orthodontics is a branch of dentistry that deals with improper tooth alignment and improper bites. Although most of our patients who visit our office are between the ages of 8 and 12 years old, we treat patients as old as age 70. I utilize braces, retainers and other devices to improve bites and tooth alignment.

Why did you choose this profession?
During my 5 years of braces, I realized that I wanted to help people and work with my hands. My orthodontist was always happy and seemed to enjoy his work.

What is interesting about your profession?
Improving smiles and improving quality of life.

What do you like most about your profession?
1. Seeing before and after pictures of treatment.
2. Making each visit fun with both kids and adults.
3. Solving different problems. Each day is unique to each patient.

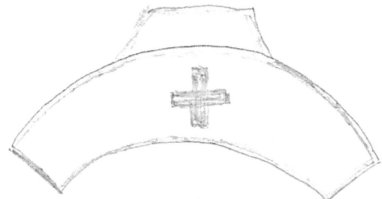

"I felt like nursing was what I was supposed to do with my life. I realized it when I was 13 and I never changed my mind."

~ MaryLisa Kissinger, R.N.

Healthcare / Nursing

MaryLisa Kissinger, R.N.
Care Manager

College/University: **Pennsylvania State University** (State College, PA)
Major: **Nursing**
Other education/certification: **Professional Registered Nurse (RN)**

Description of your profession:

Nurses help people feel better when they are sick, and stay healthy when they feel fine. There are nurses in hospitals, schools, offices, on movie sets, cruise ships, in the military, and just about anywhere you can think of. I am a Care Manager. I teach people how to get healthy and stay that way. When patients go home from the hospital, I call them and make sure they know how to take care of themselves.

Why did you choose this profession?

I wanted to matter to someone. I felt like nursing was what I was supposed to do with my life. I realized it when I was 13 and I never changed my mind.

What is interesting about your profession?

Our bodies are amazing! How is it that 2 cells, can turn into YOU, 9 months later? How does our heart remember to beat without stopping for as much as 100 years? How do you remember to breathe while you are sleeping? I learned all of that when becoming a nurse, as well as, how to help people when their bodies are ill.

What do you like most about your profession?

1. Helping someone who is afraid and sick, feel better.
2. I am able to get a job easily. I spent 8 summers in Maine as a camp nurse.
3. Every now and then, I do something that changes someone else's life for the better. There is nothing in the world like that!

Healthcare

107

"I've always wanted to be a part of a profession that helps the most vulnerable (and their families) feel better, learn more about their own health conditions, and hopefully return to better health."

~ Sharon Daniels, R.N.

Healthcare / Nursing

Sharon Daniels, R.N.
Clinical Coordinator / Nurse Educator

College/University: **Rutgers University** (New Brunswick, NJ)
Major: **Psychology, Nursing**
Other education/certification: **Professional Registered Nurse (RN), AAS - Nursing - Burlington County College** (Burlington, NJ), **BSN - Chamberlain College of Nursing** (Downing Grove, IL)

Description of your profession:
I am responsible for providing a wide range of nursing education and training to the nursing staff working in the medical and mental health areas of the 13 state prisons. I am also involved in recruiting efforts to attract quality nursing professionals to the correctional/prison setting.

Why did you choose this profession?
I have always wanted to be a part of a profession that helps the most vulnerable (and their families) feel better, learn more about their own health conditions, and hopefully return to better health.

What is interesting about your profession?
Every day is unpredictable. There is always something new to learn in the nursing field.

What do you like most about your profession?
1.   Making people laugh when they are having a bad day.
2.   Learning about new research in different areas of nursing practice.
3.   I feel like I'm really making a difference in the lives of people.

"I love fixing things and I love helping people.
Orthopedics was the perfect match for me."

~ Jason Garcia, M.D.

Healthcare / Medical

Jason Garcia, M.D.
Orthopedic Surgeon

College/University (undergraduate): **Rutgers University, Cook College** (New Brunswick, NJ)
Major: **Biological Sciences**
Medical School: **Rutgers New Jersey Medical School** (Newark, NJ)
Other education/certification: **University of California San Diego Arthroscopy and Sports Medicine Fellowship** (San Diego, CA) . **Board Certified Orthopaedic Surgeon**

Description of your profession:
I treat patients with musculoskeletal conditions including non operative and surgical management. The most common surgeries I perform are arthroscopic shoulder surgery for rotator cuff tendon tears and knee surgery for ligament, cartilage and tendon injuries.

Why did you choose this profession?
I love fixing things and I love helping people. Orthopedics was the perfect match for me.

What is interesting about your profession?
I have the ability to immediately help patients who suffer significant injuries and have pain, improve their quality of life.

What do you like most about your profession?
1.   Interacting with so many different people on a daily basis is rewarding.
2.   Operating is the most fun! That's what makes me most excited.
3.   Working with great colleagues in the office and in the operating room is fun and rewarding.

"I chose a career where I found personal satisfaction in helping communities medically and saving lives."

~ Karma Warren, M.D.

Healthcare / Medical

Karma Warren, M.D.
Assistant Professor of Emergency Medicine

College/University (undergraduate): **Tuskegee University** (Tuskegee, AL)
Major: **Electrical Engineering**
Medical School: **Rutgers, Robert Wood Johnson Medical School** (Piscataway Township, NJ)
Other education/certification: **Board Certified in Emergency Medicine**

Description of your profession:
I provide emergent medical and trauma care in the emergency room while handling EMS (Emergency Medical Services)/Medic Control Command calls. I provide conference lectures and Emergency Department bedside teaching to residents and medical students. I also advise and mentor medical students.

Why did you choose this profession?
I chose a career where I found personal satisfaction in helping communities medically and saving lives.

What is interesting about your profession?
I think it's interesting that I meet new people every day and have the opportunity to change a persons life.

What do you like most about your profession?
1. Meeting new people.
2. Saving lives.
3. Teaching new doctors to be specialist in emergency medicine.

"I knew I wanted to be a pediatric doctor from when I was 6 years old."

~ Deborah Coy, M.D.

Healthcare / Medical

Deborah Coy, M.D.
Pediatrician

College/University (undergraduate): **State University of New York at Albany** (Albany, NY)
Major: **Biology**
Medical School: **St. Georges University School of Medicine** (True Blue, Grenada)
Other education/certification: **Board Certified Pediatrician**

Description of your profession:
I am a Pediatrician who takes care of children from when they are born until they finish college. They come to see me when they are sick and even for well visits to stay healthy.

Why did you choose this profession?
I knew I wanted to be a pediatric doctor from when I was 6 years old.

What is interesting about your profession?
I love watching the children grow through all the stages of life and being an important part of it.

What do you like most about your profession?
1. Being silly with the children and feeling like I don't always have to act mature.
2. Letting the children feel comfortable and talk -- they tell you everything!
3. Having been in practice 25 years. I love that I have seen so many grow from newborn to beautiful young adults -- I now have many second generation patients.

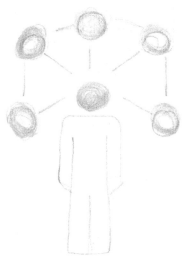

"A friend led me to Social Work. They said that talking with people and understanding them was something that was natural to me."

~ Ruth Rothbart-Mayer

Healthcare / Mental Health

Ruth Rothbart-Mayer
Psychotherapist / Elder Care Coach (Geriatric Care Manager)

College/University (undergraduate): **The College of New Jersey** (Ewing Township, NJ)
Major: **Group Work**
College/University (graduate): **Columbia University School of Social Work** (New York, NY)
MSW: **Social Work**
Other education/certification: **Certified Dementia Practitioner**

Description of your profession:
As a Psychotherapist, I work with individuals and help them identify the problems they are struggling with and help them work towards resolution and achieve greater satisfaction in life. As an Elder Care Coach, I assist families in understanding the illness one member in the family has, and what tools they need to put together a care plan.

Why did you choose this profession?
After spending years as a Speech Therapist, a friend led me to Social Work. They said that talking with people and understanding them was something that was natural to me.

What is interesting about your profession?
The opportunity to help people clarify their needs and wishes, and to provide a safe place in which to explore those emotions integral (necessary) to their well-being and growth.

What do you like most about your profession?
1. Laughing with people who at times, have forgotten how to laugh.
2. Working with lots of different people, from actors to psychiatrists to waitresses!
3. Seeing the light dawn on people's faces through their journey and finally find satisfaction or answers to problems/issues they have faced.

"I get paid doing what I love most, helping people be their best."

~ Melissa Smith

Human Resources

Melissa Smith
Vice President Human Resources

College/University: **Fairleigh Dickinson University** (Teaneck, NJ)
Major/Minor: **Sociology/Business**
Other education/certification: **Senior Human Resource Professional (SPHR)**

Description of your profession:
I work in the Human Resources department in an international food & beverage corporation. Human Resources is a department that helps companies hire people by finding talented and smart workers to perform different jobs. The Human Resources professional also makes sure people are treated fairly at work by their manager and co-workers. I help adults make smart decisions about how to work smarter and more efficiently. I provide them with the tools to help them do well in their job and make our business successful.

Why did you choose this profession?
I enjoy helping our employees bring out the best in themselves and seeing people grow within their careers.

What is interesting about your profession?
Every day is different and I have the ability to help our company be successful through the people who work here.

What do you like most about your profession?
1. Working with creative, smart and interesting people.
2. In working with a food company, there are always yummy snacks available.
3. I get paid doing what I love most, helping people be their best.

"I chose law because I find it intellectually challenging and I am interested in issues of public policy and governance."

~ Ilena Patti, Esq.

Law

Ilena Patti, Esq.
Attorney

College/University (undergraduate): **Amherst College** (Amherst, MA)
Major: **French**
Law School: **University of Michigan Law School, Juris Doctorate Degree** (Ann Arbor, MI)

Description of your profession:
I am a lawyer. Lawyers represent clients in disputes and argue particular points in issues to be decided by the courts.

Why did you choose this profession?
I chose law because I find it intellectually challenging and I am interested in issues of public policy and governance.

What is interesting about your profession?
The law is fundamental to how we choose to order and govern our society and express our values, and it is continually evolving in response to societal and technological changes.

What do you like most about your profession?
1. The intellectual challenge of dealing with complex problems.
2. The exchange of different views and interpretations of legal and policy questions.
3. Helping to solve legal problems for clients.

"I chose this profession to be the voice of the voiceless."

~ Theresa Europe, Esq.

Law

Theresa Europe, Esq.
Deputy Counsel

College/University (undergraduate): **SUNY College at Old Westbury** (Old Westbury, NY)
Major/Minor: **Business Administration/Finance**
Law School: **St. John's University School of Law, Juris Doctorate Degree** (Queens, NY)
Other education/certification: **Paralegal Certificate**

Description of your profession:
I investigate and discipline staff who engage in misconduct against children, within the one of the largest school systems in the country. I train administrators on various legal topics while increasing awareness of human trafficking of children at risk.

Why did you choose this profession?
To be the voice of the voiceless.

What is interesting about your profession?
My job brings new cases and challenges everyday.

What do you like most about your profession?
1. Interacting with and helping children.
2. Working with various District Attorney's offices in the criminal prosecution of those who commit crimes against our student population in an effort to ensure that these people are not permitted to return to teaching.
3. Speaking to students and motivating them to strive for careers in law during career day and graduation.

"I chose this profession to enjoy the two areas I love the most, law and philanthropy."

~ Monique Pryor, Esq.

Law

Monique Pryor, Esq.
Assistant Vice President of Planned Giving

College/University (undergraduate): **University of Maryland–College Park** (College Park, MD)
Major: **Journalism**
Law School: **Hofstra Law School, Juris Doctorate Degree** (Hempstead, NY)

Description of your profession:
I am a member of a fundraising organization's development team who works to cultivate (support) and manage planned giving (gifts that take planning). These gifts are usually gifts that come from a person's estate (property or possessions).

Why did you choose this profession?
To enjoy two areas I love the most, law and philanthropy.

What is interesting about your profession?
Helping Individuals use their resources to help others. Many people think they do not have the means to make significant contributions or an impact on the organization they have come to love. By educating them and connecting them with accountants and lawyers, I am able to show them how they can leave a legacy at the organizations they enjoy supporting, without paying anything out of their pocket. For example: some people do not realize that they can donate appreciated stock to a charity. The donor is able to avoid capital gains tax and receive an immediate charitable deduction while supporting the institution.

What do you like most about your profession?
1. Meeting interesting people.
2. Seeing people and programs transform because of the generosity of others.
3. Helping others realize their giving potential.

125

"I decided to be a lawyer because I love to read, write and solve problems."

~ Kayleigh Pettit, Esq.

Law

Kayleigh Pettit, Esq.
Senior Counsel

College/University (undergraduate): **University of Maryland--College Park** (College Park, MD)
Major/Minor: **English Language and Literature, Concentration in Rhetoric**
Law School: **Brooklyn Law School, Juris Doctorate Degree** (Brooklyn, NY)

Description of your profession:
I am a contracts lawyer. Meaning, I spend my days reading, writing and negotiating contracts. I make money for and protect my company through the words in our contracts.

Why did you choose this profession?
I decided to be a lawyer because I love to read, write and solve problems.

What is interesting about your profession?
I enjoy working together with lawyers from other companies to make important deals happen.

What do you like most about your profession?
1.	Working on deals with cool and interesting companies.
2.	Working with people from around the world.
3.	I have an office in Times Square!

"I chose this profession to be able to work in a rapidly expanding area of law."

~ Ebonee Lewis, Esq.

Law

Ebonee Lewis, Esq.
Senior Employment Counsel

College/University (undergraduate): Syracuse University (Syracuse, NY)
Major: Political Science
Law School: Georgetown University Law Center, Juris Doctorate Degree (Washington, DC)

Description of your profession:
I am primarily responsible for providing employment law advise and guidance to various business units and global functions at my company. Additionally, I am responsible for managing outside counsel's handling of employment-related litigation (legal action) matters.

Why did you choose this profession?
To be able to work in a rapidly expanding area of the law.

What is interesting about your profession?
The practice of employment law is all about people and their relationships in the workplace.

What do you like most about your profession?
1. My work is always exciting; it's never dull.
2. Working with a great team of other women attorneys.
3. I travel to interesting places like, Colorado Springs, CO; Beverly Hills, CA and San Juan, Puerto Rico.

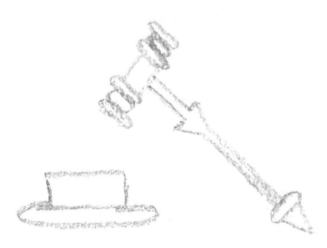

"My mom is a lawyer and retired judge. Growing up, I saw how so many relied on her knowledge, so I decided I also wanted to be the "go to" girl for all things legal."

~ Kecia Clarke, Esq.

Law / Entertainment

Kecia Clarke, Esq.
Attorney / Author / Entrepreneur

College/University (undergraduate): **Rutgers University, Rutgers College** (New Brunswick, NJ)
Major: **Criminal Justice**
Law School: **Seton Hall University School of Law, Juris Doctorate Degree** (Newark, NJ)
Other education/certification: **Interior Design certification**

Description of your profession:
As an attorney and lifestyle entrepreneur, I appear on TV and speak at events where I share how my legal expertise has catapulted (launched) me into branding myself as a lifestyle entrepreneur with six books under my belt, and currently writing my 7th, on the benefits of being a lifestyle entrepreneur.

Why did you choose this profession?
My mom is a lawyer and retired judge. Growing up, I saw how so many relied on her knowledge, so I decided I also wanted to be the "go to" girl for all things legal.

What is interesting about your profession?
The fact the law affects everybody. At some point, everybody needs a lawyer – for the good and the bad. My law degree allows me to say loudly, "I will always have a job!" Amazing!

What do you like most about your profession?
1. Appearing on TV discussing current legal/pop culture topics.
2. Winning a case against a not so nice adversary! Being a lawyer has some power. We think we know it all and people listen to us! And, we are right most times!
3. Being a lifestyle entrepreneur allows me to work from anywhere...literally.

"I chose law enforcement because it is a rewarding and challenging profession."

~ Eleazar Ricardo

Law Enforcement

Eleazar Ricardo
Lieutenant of County Detectives

College/University: **New Jersey City University** (Jersey City, NJ)
Major: **Criminal Justice**
Other education/certification: **Police Academy**

Description of your profession:
I am currently in charge of the Major Crimes Unit for a large county. We investigate all homicides and suspicious death within the county.

Why did you choose this profession?
I chose law enforcement because it is a rewarding and challenging profession and I didn't want to work sitting in an office.

What is interesting about your profession?
My actions can have a positive or negative consequence for people.

What do you like most about your profession?
1. Helping others in doing something that makes their life a little easier is fun. Such as, helping someone with directions or directing traffic to make the commute easier.
2. There are many training courses that you have to go through that are fun; vehicle pursuit, defensive tactics, interview, community policing and much more!
3. The camaraderie. Work in law enforcement offers a sense of belonging and family that you would not find in other careers. Your co-workers are your extended family and your partner is like the brother or sister you never had.

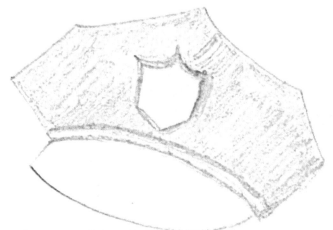

"This unique position in law enforcement allows me to educate, empower and encourage those who have made past mistakes, learn strategies to make the right decisions."

~ Tamaira Wilkes

Law Enforcement

Tamaira Wilkes
Senior Parole Officer

College/University: **Rutgers University** (New Brunswick, NJ)
Major: **Administration of Justice**
Other education/certification: **Police Training Commission Certified**

Description of your profession:

I supervise individuals who were convicted of a crime and served time in prison, who are released back into the community, but have not completed their sentence. This includes providing them with re-entry needs, such as employment and counseling, in efforts to help them become productive members of society and to not re-offend. I also protect the community by ensuring that the general and special conditions that they must adhere to, are being followed, and take action to keep them in compliance, or invoke graduated sanctions including re-incarceration when violations occur.

Why did you choose this profession?

When I was in 7th grade, I became acutely aware of the power you can have by knowing your rights, following rules, and making the right decisions. This unique position in law enforcement allows me to educate, empower and encourage those who have made past mistakes, learn strategies to make the right decisions.

What is interesting about your profession?

I find the study of human behavior to be most interesting.

What do you like most about your profession?

1. I have made lasting relationships with my partners and co-workers.
2. Helping people and using my problem solving and decision making skill set.
3. Meeting, helping and relating to new people all of the time.

Thought Bubble Tips

Thought Bubble Tips

Refer to the thought bubble tips regularly.

1. Imagine

2. Passion

3. Visualize

4. Goals

5. Read

6. Grades

7. Practice

8. Encourage

9. Lead

10. Mentor

11. Shadow

12. Volunteer

13. Network

14. Happy

Thought Bubble Tips are on pages 9 – 37.

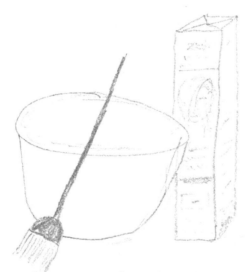

"There is nothing more fun than being your own boss."

~ Albert Eric Celleri

Manufacturing

Albert Eric Celleri
Chief Operating Officer

College/University: **Bloomsburg University** (Bloomsburg, PA)
Major: **Economics**

Description of your profession:
I am a full service provider of hair dye raw materials, technical services and education to the hair color industry.

Why did you choose this profession?
I was exposed to the hair dye industry at the age of 16 while working for my father's company and eventually found it to be a challenging industry that I wanted to take on.

What is interesting about your profession?
The most interesting aspect of my profession is that it is highly specialized and rare.

What do you like most about your profession?
1.	My job affords me the opportunity to travel the world. I have traveled to Jakarta, Indonesia – Ho Chi Minh City, Vietnam -- and Johannesburg, South Africa, just to name a few.
2.	The prospect of innovating new products and setting hair fashion trends.
3.	There is nothing more fun than being your own boss.

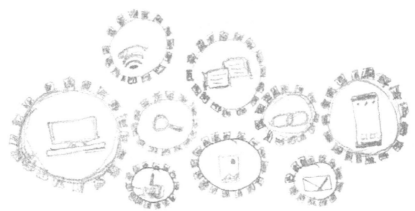

"Marketing is a job that allows you to be creative, use color, imagine, talk to people, think up new ways of communicating; and I love that there is variety and it is fun!"

~ Amy Scott

Marketing

Amy Scott
Vice President of Marketing

College/University (undergraduate): **Indiana University** (Bloomington, IN)
Major/Minor: **Business/Psychology**
College/University (graduate): **Pepperdine University** (Malibu, CA)
MBA: **Master of Business Administration**

Description of your profession:
I get to create the name for a product, what the packaging will look like, how to make it sound like something people want to buy, set the price they will have to pay, figure out how to advertise so they can learn about it, decide if I advertise on TV, online, or some other way, and measure how many products are sold over time.

Why did you choose this profession?
Marketing is a job that allows you to be creative, use color, imagine, talk to people, think up new ways of communicating; and I love that there is variety and it is fun!

What is interesting about your profession?
I can use social media and the internet to let people know about my product in a way that makes them want to learn more and purchase it .

What do you like most about your profession?
1. Interacting with a lot of people inside and outside of the company daily.
2. Thinking about different ways to solve problems and get more sales.
3. Every day is very different, so I never get bored!

"I chose marketing because of the endless opportunities to be creative and think outside of the box."

~ Janelle Mitchell

Marketing

Janelle Mitchell
Sales Marketing Manager

College/University: **North Carolina A&T State University** (Greensboro, NC)
Major: **Marketing**

Description of your profession:
My company provides millions of images, video clips, music tracks and editorial content, which is used by both big and small businesses, marketing agencies and media organizations around the world. In my role, I am responsible for communicating the value of my company to brands and advertising agencies through a variety of marketing channels.

Why did you choose this profession?
I chose marketing because of the endless opportunities to be creative and think outside of the box.

What is interesting about your profession?
The way people consume information is constantly changing which means that we frequently come up with new ways to market our products and services.

What do you like most about your profession?
1. I get to work with a lot of different departments at my company, therefore, I am able to develop relationships with a variety of people.
2. Brainstorming and coming up with new ways to market our products and services to our clients.
3. Traveling and attending industry events that allow me to interact with people who use our content. It's great hearing about how they love our content!

"I get a chance to sit with music artists and discuss creative digital marketing ideas that will help them gain fans and spread their music to the world."

~ Kathy Baker

Digital Marketing

Kathy Baker
Senior Vice President, Digital Marketing

College/University: **Rutgers University, College of Engineering** (New Brunswick, NJ)
Major: **Mechanical Engineering**
Other education/certification: **Certificate in Internet/Intranet Management and Design from Columbia University** (New York, NY)

Description of your profession:
I am responsible for leading digital strategy including social media and content marketing, online advertising, mobile marketing, customer relationship management, and emerging technology for over 100 recording artists at the #1 record label in the music industry.

Why did you choose this profession?
I enjoy being on the cutting edge of technology while using my strong analytical and creative marketing skills.

What is interesting about your profession?
My job is constantly changing as technology emerges and becomes useful for our marketing strategies.

What do you like most about your profession?
1.   I get a chance to sit with music artists and discuss creative digital marketing ideas that will help them to gain fans and spread their music to the world.
2.   Attending concerts and shows for all of our artists, sometimes many times per week.
3.   Visiting the offices of our favorite social media companies!

"I chose this profession because I enjoy marketing and digital technology."

~ Abigail Elsmore

Digital Marketing

Abigail Elsmore
Email Production Coordinator

College/University: **Katherine Gibbs School** (Montclair, NJ)
Major: **Secretarial Arts/Associates Degree**

Description of your profession:
I am responsible for the email production process, including client relations, list targeting, html coding, email testing and troubleshooting for a large publishing company.

Why did you choose this profession?
I chose this profession because I enjoy marketing and digital technology.

What is interesting about your profession?
In this role, I am always learning new and exciting changes in the digital world.

What do you like most about your profession?
1. Keeping current on digital platforms and web based marketing tools for email blasts, e-newsletters and website ad serving.
2. Creating list strategies (deciding which consumers will receive certain emails) to help marketing campaigns succeed.
3. I enjoy the friendships I make through client contacts and co-workers.

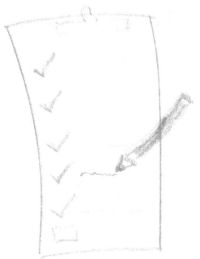

"I love working with people and coordinating events."

~ Maxine Gooden

Event Marketing

Maxine Gooden
Event Planner

College/University: **Parsons School of Design** (New York, NY)
Major/Minor: **Architectural/Interior**
Other education/certification: **Project Management Certification**

Description of your profession:
As an Event Planner, I manage an event from beginning to end. I meet with clients and their teams to discuss their event needs. I plan the event details and work within an established budget. I look for and book locations, caterers, entertainment and staff.

Why did you choose this profession?
I love working with people and coordinating events.

What is interesting about your profession?
No event is the same. You never know what to expect.

What do you like most about your profession?
1. Meeting new people and interacting with them gives me the opportunity to learn about what people enjoy doing when they are not working.
2. Traveling allows me to learn more about the city I am visiting.
3. Working various events like trade shows, corporate events and fundraisers from concept to completion.

"I have a passion for creating awesome consumer experiences and I love building events from concept to completion."

~ Andrea Lokshin

Event Marketing

Andrea Lokshin
Vice President of Sales & Marketing

College/University: **University of Hartford** (West Hartford, CT)
Major/Minor: **Marketing/Communications**
Other education/certification: **Mini MBA Digital Marketing - Rutgers School of Business**
(New Brunswick, NJ)

Description of your profession:
I work in the Marketing department of a large entertainment venue, which is also a landmark location. I drive revenue (increase business and sales) and create stronger marketing and branding, so that my facility becomes a true destination for private, public and corporate events.

Why did you choose this profession?
I have a passion for creating awesome consumer experiences and I love building events from concept to completion.

What is interesting about your profession?
The opportunity to be a part of re-building a landmark location.

What do you like most about your profession?
1. Driving new revenue opportunities by leveraging (using) my extensive database of contacts.
2. The ability to apply creative details to make events extra special.
3. Enjoying endless events that the venue has to offer with my friends and family.

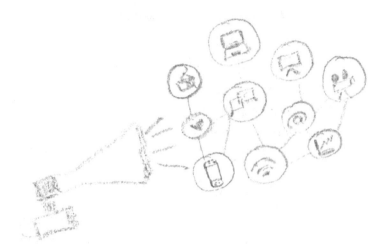

"I fell in love with advertising when I was a kid watching a Bill Cosby television commercial."

~ Audrey De Shong

Integrated Marketing

Audrey De Shong
Director of Integrated Marketing

College/University: **Bloomfield College** (Bloomfield, NJ)
Major/Minor: **Industrial, Organizational Psychology/Marketing**

Description of your profession:
I oversee creative strategy and development from conception through execution for brand campaigns for one of the nation's premier retailers. I also manage communications for all cross-functional teams (legal, creative, production, media and visual). My responsibility on any shoot, is to ensure that the Director and art direction is being met to meet the creative concept (idea), and to ensure all the details being filmed, align with the brand as well.

Why did you choose this profession?
I fell in love with advertising when I was a kid watching a Bill Cosby television commercial. At that moment, I knew I wanted to somehow work in Advertising/Marketing.

What is interesting about your profession?
It is dynamic and diverse, as I am always working on new ideas with lots of people.

What do you like most about your profession?
1.   There is a wide range of developing new content (from TV to social media to in-store). It challenges me to think and grow with each new program that I develop.
2.   I enjoy working with fun and smart people. I have also filmed a few great celebrities like Usher, Taylor Swift, Carlos Santana and many more!
3.   No shoot is ever the same. I've been blessed and have filmed all over the U.S. and Canada!

"After conducting my first "reporting" project for a class in college, I began to imagine a profession in television and sports."

~ Angela Vrtis

Media

Angela Vrtis
Director of Sales

College/University: **Montana State University Billings** (Billings, MT)
Major: **Communications**

Description of your profession:
I sell advertising for television commercials.

Why did you choose this profession?
When I was in college, I took a class on television and media. After conducting my first "reporting" project for the class, I began to imagine a profession in television and sports. I decided to become a writer, reporting sports stories for a newspaper... after all, I loved to write and I loved sports! A few years later, I began working for a company and got many opportunities within the company to work my way from librarian to a video marketing manager and then to sales. It really pays to dream about what you want to do in your life and then work hard toward that goal!

What is interesting about your profession?
I love working with different people in different markets. There are so many interesting cities and each have their own unique personalities.

What do you like most about your profession?
1.   Traveling to lots of sporting events and big cities all over the country!
2.   Meeting people from many different cities.
3.   It is exciting to negotiate with clients and make deals that work for both companies.

"I've always wanted to make movies. I went to school for it and was able to do it once I graduated."

~ Justin Lundstrom

Media

Justin Lundstrom
Head of Programming & Production

College/University: **Keene State College** (Keene, New Hampshire)
Major/Minor: **Film Production/Film Criticism**

Description of your profession:
Any company will have a plan or mission. In my position, I take the company mission and create a plan to make videos that fit in with the plan/mission. Then, I oversee how the videos will be made and hire the people to make them the way I need them made. I see the process all the way through to the end. I also take part in the way the videos are put up on the internet or if it's a movie, where we want the movie showing, and if it is TV, I'd think of which network would be best for the company's mission.

Why did you choose this profession?
I've always wanted to make movies. I went to school for It, was able to do it once I graduated, and have been able to transition into video production, where the need is very high right now.

What is interesting about your profession?
I use my taste, style and personality to communicate through video to an audience.

What do you like most about your profession?
1. Traveling to all kinds of cities/countries like Milan, Italy - Vancouver, Canada - and Helsinki, Finland. I'm in Los Angeles and Las Vegas at least once a month.
2. Choosing the topics for videos that people will make and other people will watch.
3. Being on the set shooting videos, determining where the camera will go, working with the people who will be on camera, and more!

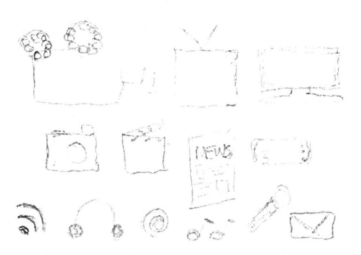

"I like the challenge of sales and the gratification of closing deals that are mutually beneficial for the network and the client."

~ Ann McCarron

Media

Ann McCarron
Senior Vice President, Advertising Sales

College/University: **Rutgers University** (New Brunswick, NJ)
Double Major: **Exercise Science/Sports Studies and Dance**
Other education/certification: **IAB Digital Sales Certified**

Description of your profession:
I oversee a team that is responsible for selling advertising time, media sponsorships and program integrations for a major network, cable networks, digital sites and partnerships. When you see a commercial on a TV network or on a digital site, there are people who buy and sell the space on the channel in which you see the commercial. Therefore, when you see a commercial on my network, my team sold the space to that advertiser.

Why did you choose this profession?
I like the challenge of sales and the gratification of closing deals that are mutually beneficial for the network and the client.

What is interesting about your profession?
I get to work with great brands of the biggest, most credible, respected and innovative media company in the world.

What do you like most about your profession?
1.   Going to concerts every week in the summer and starting my day off with a live concert performed by the most popular musical acts.
2.   Meeting interesting and smart people, including news talent, producers, advertising agency executives and clients who make me smarter.
3.   Learning about the latest innovations in media and how we can use them in our sales.

159

"I chose a profession in Broadcast Media because I loved to watch television as a child."

~ Candace Green

Media

Candace Green
Director, Research and Marketing

College/University: **Hampton University** (Hampton, VA)
Major: **Marketing**

Description of your profession:
I interpret television ratings and other data to uncover information about a television program and its viewers. This information lets me know how many people watched a television program, who these people are, where they live, what they like to do in their spare time and what they like to buy. I provide this information to the people who create the television programs, sell the commercial airtime and the advertisers who buy commercials that air during the television programs.

Why did you choose this profession?
I chose a profession in Broadcast Media because I loved to watch television as a child.

What is interesting about your profession?
I get to understand why television viewers like or dislike a television program.

What do you like most about your profession?
1. Previewing new television programs before they air on TV.
2. Creating stories about what type of television programs people watch and put it into a PowerPoint presentation.
3. I get to talk to advertisers about why it is important for their commercial to air during a specific television program, because millions of people watch the program, and those people will most likely watch their commercial and be convinced to buy the product or service.

"I found something that I feel passionate about and it doesn't feel like work."

~ Donnie Campbell

Media

Donnie Campbell
Chief Executive Officer / Founder

College/University: **St. Louis University** (St. Louis, MO)
Major/Minor: **Computer Science/Math**

Description of your profession:
I created a media company which gives exposure to athletes. My primary role is to create an environment where my team, my company and I, think big, dream, inspire, lead, innovate and enable change.

Why did you choose this profession?
I found something that I feel passionate about and it doesn't feel like work. My dream is to help others reach their dreams and my company is allowing me to do just that.

What is interesting about your profession?
Working with so many people in the sports industry, from athletes to executives..

What do you like most about your profession?
1. As a successful entrepreneur, you can pick who you work with, when you work, where you work, and how you work.
2. Working hard and working smart are often rewarded in the currency that is important to you.
3. I get to make fun decisions like naming my company and picking the color of the logo.

"I have made this my life's mission and no longer consider this to be a dream deferred, instead the dream realized."

~ Reggie Miller

Motivational Speaker / Community Activist

Reggie Miller
Program Director, Male Student Support Program

College/University: **Rutgers University** (New Brunswick, NJ)
Major: **Sociology**

Description of your profession:
I lead a program in the community that addresses the psychosocial challenges impacting male students. I inspire and encourage others to be the best they can be, through presentations and motivational speeches, based on practical experiences.

Why did you choose this profession?
I dreamed of playing professional basketball. As a 6.5 Guard, I was accepted into a division one athletic program with a full scholarship to play, however, one day in practice I landed wrong, was rushed to the hospital, and the doctors discovered I had spinal stenosis. Just like that, my dream ended and I did not have a plan for the dream deferred. When I graduated from college, I had no idea what I wanted to do. Going back home, I started to see where my community lacked compared to other communities. The community needed someone who would inspire them to dream bigger than their circumstance to build a better future. The ones who needed to hear that message the most were the youth. I have made this my life's mission and no longer consider this to be a dream deferred, instead the dream realized.

What is interesting about your profession?
The ability to make a difference in the life of someone else.

What do you like most about your profession?
1.   Interacting with the students and hearing about what's going on in their lives.
2.   Being able to direct or provide helpful resources to students.
3.   Giving back to my community.

165

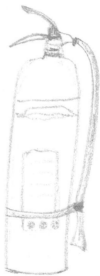

"I felt like if I shared my personal experiences, I could help educate and inspire young adults."

~ Shawn Simons

Motivational Speaker

Shawn Simons
Motivational Speaker

College/University: **Seton Hall University** (South Orange, NJ)
Major: **Business Management**

Description of your profession:
I talk to young adults about having survived a fire while I was in college. I teach fire safety and speak about overcoming tragedy. I've also contributed to writing a book and written several articles. My job allows me to educate, inspire and speak in front of thousands of people.

Why did you choose this profession?
I felt like if I shared my personal experiences, I could help educate and inspire young adults.

What is interesting about your profession?
I get a chance to share my story with close to 50,000 people a year.

What do you like most about your profession?
1. Traveling within the United States and all around the world, to places like Dubai and Abu Dhabi, United Emirates - Bali, Indonesia - Mexico, Dominican Republic, Jamaica, Curacao, Puerto Rico, St. Johns and Belize, to name a few.
2. I make my own schedule.
3. Helping people by inspiring them to never give up.

"Jazz allows for expression of ideas that cannot always be expressed in words."

~ Isaiah J. Thompson

Music

Isaiah J. Thompson
Student

College/University: **The Juilliard School** (New York, NY)
Major: **Jazz Piano**

Description of your profession:
I am an aspiring Jazz Musician.

Why did you choose this profession?
I love music, but I think jazz is an art form that is at times, under appreciated.

What is interesting about your profession?
My profession is interesting because no one does it the same. There are some values that have to be there, each time, in order for jazz to still be jazz. Improvisation is key.

What do you like most about your profession?
1. The art form is very creative and allows people to explore their own personalities through the music.
2. Jazz is a social art form that requires people to come together to create something new. I've had the opportunity to perform with some amazing musicians in some cool venues in the United States and around the world, including: Santa Cruz, Bolivia ~ Lima and Cusco, Peru ~ Bern and Geneva, Switzerland ~ Groznjan, Croatia ~ Weikersheim, Germany ~ Trieste, Italy ~ Brussels, Belgium and Copenhagen, Denmark.
3. Jazz allows for expression of ideas that cannot always be expressed in words.

GOAL

"I like witnessing the work that I perform affect
positively a population of people in the community."

~ Deborah Hurley

Non-Profit Organization

Deborah Hurley
Director of Advancement and Communication

College/University: **Marymount College** (New York, NY)
Major/Minor: **Political Science/Sociology**

Description of your profession:
I am responsible for raising $2 million a year and making sure that our marketing and communications is effective statewide.

Why did you choose this profession?
I truly stumbled upon my industry. I went to college to become a news reporter and ended up enjoying advocacy work and politics. As a result, I interned on Capitol Hill, securing a job later working for a Congressman. I then landed a job fundraising for elected officials which then turned into fundraising for a not-for-profit organization.

What is interesting about your profession?
I meet the most interesting people who are very resourceful, successful, and influential. And then, I meet that person who is just truly passionate about the issue before them, and would give their last dollar to see the organization do well – and it is usually that person who does not have the means or resources.

What do you like most about your profession?
1. Meeting new people.
2. Witnessing the work that I perform, affect positively a population of people in the community, access to more resources (i.e., food, education, housing and more!).
3. Becoming a mentor. In this industry, someone always latches onto you, and you eventually are able to give back easily and help a person grow/succeed.

171

"I love working with young people and wanted to make a positive impact on peoples lives."

~ Theodore Simmons

Non-Profit Organization

Theodore Simmons
Director of Student Ministries

College/University: **Messiah College** (Mechanicsburg, PA)
Major: **Nursing**

Description of your profession:
I work in a church setting with students between 6th and 12th grade. It is my job to build an exciting, creative, welcoming and fun atmosphere, in order to teach various topics teenagers have questions about, so that they can ultimately grow in their lives with God.

Why did you choose this profession?
I love working with young people and wanted to make a positive impact on peoples lives.

What is interesting about your profession?
I have the ability to make a difference in hundreds of peoples lives.

What do you like most about your profession?
1. Getting to know so many interesting people.
2. Planning and going on exciting trips: retreats, amusement parks, concerts and more!
3. I get to teach within the church.

"I like being able to create things that improve the school and watch those improvements happen from start to finish."

~ Robert Elsmore

Operations Management

Robert Elsmore
Director of Plant Operations

College/University: **William Paterson University** (Wayne, NJ)
Major/Minor: **Liberal Arts**
Other education/certification: **Rutgers University** (New Brunswick, NJ) – Education Facility
Management, Emergency Management, Asbestos Management, Indoor Air Quality (IAQ),
Integrated Pest Management, Transportation Director, Certified Pool Operator.

Description of your profession:
I supervise jobs related to the mechanical and physical maintenance and repairs of
schools.

Why did you choose this profession?
I chose this job to work in my community and be a part of the education system in
my hometown.

What is interesting about your profession?
Seeing the huge support system that makes schools safe for the students to attend.

What do you like most about your profession?
1. The interaction with parents, students and teachers daily, many of whom I
    know from my community.
2. The involvement with all of the athletic teams and improvement of the
    facilities, fields and gymnasiums they use.
3. Being able to create things that improve the school and watch those
    improvements happen from start to finish.

"The reality is, I did not choose this profession. God chose me!"

~ Pastor Da'rryl Hall

Pastor

Da'rryl Hall
Senior Pastor

College/University: **Charleston Southern University** (Charleston, SC)
Major/Minor: **Marketing/Economics**

Description of your profession:
To teach and preach the word of God, and lead God's people in the direction God would have us go, based on his word.

Why did you choose this profession?
The reality is, I did not choose this profession. God chose me!

What is interesting about your profession?
I still get amazed at how God still uses me with my imperfections.

What do you like most about your profession?
1. I enjoy preaching to different Congregations (group of people assembled for religious worship).
2. Traveling all over to Minister. I've been to many cities in the U.S. and I've been to Eldoret and Narobi, Africa.
3. Counseling individuals and couples and seeing them become successful.

"My mother took me to see a Broadway show when I was 7 years old and I fell I love with the theater."

~ Marlaina Powell

Performing Arts

Marlaina Powell
Singer and Actress

College/University (undergraduate): **Howard University** (NW Washington, DC) **/CUNY BA** (NY, NY)
Major/Minor: **Classical Voice and Musical Theater**
College/University (graduate): **New York University – Steinhardt** (New York, NY)
MM: **Master of Music – Concentration in Vocal Performance**

Description of your profession:
I am a professional singer and actress who has worked on Broadway, in regional theaters and as a backup singer for major label artists including Bebe Winans, Yolanda Adams, Chaka Khan and Oleta Adams.

Why did you choose this profession?
My mother took me to see a Broadway show when I was 7 years old and I fell in love with the theater.

What is interesting about your profession?
The most interesting thing about being a performing artist is working with all types of people.

What do you like most about your profession?
1. I have so much fun singing. It is like breathing to me.
2. My schedule is very flexible and is ever-changing. I am not and never have been a morning person. I love being able to work at night (most of the time).
3. Playing different characters. In one show, I might be a nurse or a teacher, and in the next one, a police officer or a witch.

"I chose to run for Mayor so that I could make a difference."

~ Mayor Nathaniel Anderson

Politics

Nathaniel Anderson
Mayor

College/University: **Fairleigh Dickinson University** (Teaneck, NJ)
Major: **Business Management**

Description of your profession:
As the head of the city, the Mayor officially speaks for both the government and the community as a whole. In all statutory cities, the Mayor is the presiding officer and a regular member of the city council. Being Mayor is a high-profile position, with plenty of interaction with both government officials and the community. Mayors typically run their city and work with the legislative body to enact laws. They preside over council meetings, provide leadership, receive input from constituents (voters) and make business decisions.

Why did you choose this profession?
I chose to run for Mayor so that I could make a difference. So many people complain about issues, but they don't do anything to be a part of the solution. I believe that you have to be at the table in order to have your voice heard.

What is interesting about your profession?
Some of my responsibilities as a Mayor are ensuring the streets are plowed during the winter, making sure our infrastructure is in good condition, finding ways to stabilize taxes and making sure there are quality of life programs for our seniors and the community. Most policy decisions come down to a vote from the full council.

What do you like most about your profession?
1. Helping people and making them smile.
2. Meeting other influential politicians.
3. Going on ride-alongs with the police and fire departments.

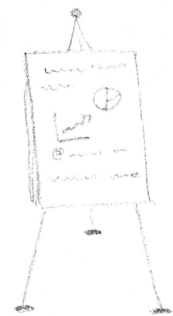

"I like working with abstract concepts and ideas, and turning them into actionable plans."

~ Marcia Porchia

Project Management

Marcia Porchia
Senior Director, Project Management Office

College/University: **University of Arkansas** (Fayetteville, AR)
Major: **Computer Information Systems**
Other education/certification: **Project Management Professional (PMP), Advanced Project Management Certification**

Description of your profession:
I am responsible for aligning organizational strategy to business outcomes through the execution of projects. Meaning, I take the leaders vision and put plans in place to make it happen.

Why did you choose this profession?
I like working with abstract concepts and ideas, and turning them into actionable plans. I chose this position so I could have visibility into where the company is headed and directly contribute to the success.

What is interesting about your profession?
Every project that I work on is unique in terms of impact to the business, therefore, I learn something new all of the time.

What do you like most about your profession?
1.   Working in a team oriented environment.
2.   Learning new aspects of the business.
3.   Celebrating the success at the end.

"I enjoy negotiating, selling and closing deals."

~ David Oliver

Real Estate / Media

David Oliver
Real Estate Broker / Franchise Owner / Coach

College/University: **Charleston Southern University** (Charleston, SC)
Major/Minor: **History/Criminal Justice**
Other education/certification: **Real Estate Broker License**

Description of your profession:

I own and operate a real estate business. As a Real Estate Broker, I market and sell residential and commercial properties, and supervise the Realtors in my office. I am also a franchise owner of a sports media company. In this role, I work with sports executives and provide a way to help gain exposure for young athletes. In my spare time, I enjoy coaching basketball.

Why did you choose this profession?

My mother had an interest in real estate, which gave me exposure to the industry early on. A few years after college, I had the opportunity to start a real estate business and I went for it. I enjoy negotiating, selling and closing deals. I also have a passion for basketball, and coaching this sport is fulfilling to me.

What is interesting about your profession?

Meeting new people and finding them the property of their dreams.

What do you like most about your profession?

1. As a Real Estate Broker, I enjoy closing deals.
2. As a franchise owner, I like traveling to different sports venues.
3. As a basketball coach, I like working with young athletes and seeing them grow in the sport.

"I've always had a passion for knowing the latest trends and shopping at various stores for good deals."

~ Candice Hardiman

Retail / Merchandising

Candice Hardiman
Buyer / Category Manager

College/University: **University of Missouri – Columbia** (Columbia, MO)
Major: **Business Administration**

Description of your profession:
I buy and help design products to sell in retail stores and online. I am responsible for finding the right product for the right price in the right stores. I work with vendors to select the product and negotiate the best cost so that I can sell it in stores at a profit. My job is to make the shopping experience enjoyable for the customer and show great value. So when you go to a store, Buyers decide what you can buy and at what price.

Why did you choose this profession?
I've always had a passion for knowing the latest trends and shopping at various stores for good deals. I always wanted to be a Buyer because I love to shop and I love to sell items and make money. My passion started when I had my first lemonade stand and I sold tons of lemonade to friends in the neighborhood.

What is interesting about your profession?
It is exciting to see customers with an item you put in the store or featured online.

What do you like most about your profession?
1. Traveling around the world to find the right products for the customers. I've been to Shenzhen, China~ Florence, Italy~ Barcelona, Spain~ Antwerp, Belgium~ Kowloon, Hong Kong~ Frankfurt, Germany~ Amsterdam, Netherlands~ London, England and Paris, France.
2. Working with several other teams (marketing, sales, financial and inventory planners, designers and vendors) to get the job done.
3. I get a report card (sales & profit) and learn from opportunities and celebrate my success!

Retail

"I get extremely excited when I see people wearing or using products that I've created or brought to market."

~ Kimberly Lee Minor

Fashion/Retail & Branding

Kimberly Lee Minor
Senior Vice President, Home Fashion & Retail Operations

College/University (undergraduate): **Temple University** (Philadelphia, PA)
Major/Minor: **Radio, Television, Film/Dance, Speech, Art**
College/University (graduate): **Drexel University** (Philadelphia, PA)
MBA: **Master of Business Administration – Concentration in Marketing**

Description of your profession:
I lead the teams that create the products, set the price, and present the products in stores for your enjoyment and consumption. Currently, those products are candles, home fragrance and décor. In my career, I have done women's, kid's and men's fashion apparel, accessories, bridal apparel, athletic apparel and footwear.

Why did you choose this profession?
It chose me! I entered in to the executive training program of one of the nation's largest retailers, where I learned the art and science of fashion, and was hooked by the fact that I could still be a part of people's lives by influencing their purchase habits.

What is interesting about your profession?
I spend a large amount of time learning who my customer is and what she/he needs or wants, so that I win the daily challenge of insuring that it is created and available.

What do you like most about your profession?
1. Traveling the world to see what other creative business people are offering their customers!
2. I get extremely excited when I see people wearing or using products that I've created or brought to market.
3. Meeting my customers is so much fun! They tell me the truth – good and bad!

189

"My acquisition of the company enables me to help people overcome their everyday hair challenges and to build a legacy in the community of color."

~ Renee Rhoten Morris

Retail

Renee Rhoten Morris
Chief Curl Officer

College/University (undergraduate): **Dillard University** (New Orleans, LA)
Major/Minor: **Accounting/English**
College/University (graduate): **Ross School of Business: University of Michigan** (Ann Arbor, MI)
MBA: **Master of Business Administration - Concentration in Strategy**

Description of your profession:
I am the Chief Curl Officer of a global beauty company. My goal is to educate and inspire women, men and children who choose to wear their hair naturally. I work to design all-natural solutions that meet the need of every curl pattern. My products are distributed in over 3,000 stores globally, including several major retailers. To ensure our success, I partner with people all over the world, from social media influencers to raw material suppliers to supply chain experts. I am involved in every aspect of our business.

Why did you choose this profession?
I don't think I chose this profession, but rather God showed it to me. I acquired (bought/obtained) the company after deciding to leave my 20+ year career in management consulting. I personally used the product on my hair, and discovered there was an opportunity to acquire the brand after visiting the local store to replenish my supply.

What is interesting about your profession?
The ability to revert back to being in high school – talking about and playing with hair all day.

What do you like most about your profession?
1. Thinking about solutions that solve the problems of people with natural hair.
2. Attending events where I help women and girls learn about their hair.
3. Looking at beautiful pictures of women and girls who do amazing things with their hair.

191

"I chose this profession because I believe it represents the highest and best use of the qualities God gave me."

~ Holly St. Clair

Sales / Healthcare

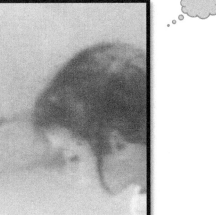

Holly St. Clair
Physician Services – Stereotactic Radiosurgery

College/University: **Villanova University** (Villanova, PA)
Major/Minor: **Communication/Sociology**

Description of your profession:
I educate physicians on radiosurgery (surgery utilizing radiation) for the treatment of benign and malignant tumors. My interactions with doctors include listening so that I can understand what types of patients they are treating, and helping them identify patients that are candidates for radiosurgery.

Why did you choose this profession?
I chose this profession because I believe it represents the highest and best use of the qualities God gave me. I chose an education in Communications because I believe that many disagreements stem from miscommunications, and I wanted to learn more about how to communicate appropriately in efforts to avoid misunderstandings. Equally, I wanted to better understand the human behaviors.

What is interesting about your profession?
I am amazed when I speak to cancer patients who have a positive and bright outlook on life, despite the health issues they are facing. I believe mindset and attitude are important in achieving the desired outcome.

What do you like most about your profession?
1. Human interaction and meeting new people.
2. Creating programs to help people gain an understanding of their treatment options.
3. Every day brings new challenges and new experiences that I am learning from.

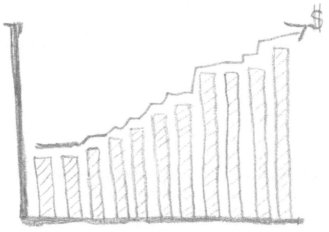

"I chose this profession because as a little girl, I won
a trophy for selling the most cookies in my troop."

~ Shirelle Whitaker Howze

Sales / Business Development

Shirelle Whitaker Howze
Sales Representative

College/University: **University of Maryland – College Park** (College Park, MD)
Major/Minor: **Criminal Justice/Psychology**
Other education/certification: **Leadership Training**

Description of your profession:
I identify sales and marketing business opportunities for new and existing businesses. I sell products by developing relationships with customers and recommending solutions to help grow the customer and company's market share.

Why did you choose this profession?
I chose this profession because as a little girl, I won a trophy for selling the most cookies in my troop. I always enjoyed helping people, offering advice, introducing new products, promotions and the ability to make unlimited money.

What is interesting about your profession?
This profession has no limits. It allows you to make a difference in meeting the customers needs. You must be self confident, committed, disciplined, knowledgeable, honest and enthusiastic.

What do you like most about your profession?
1. Travelling and the ability to negotiate and close the deal.
2. Meeting lots of different people with various ethnicities and backgrounds.
3. I enjoy the company's perks (corporate credit card and company car) and networking with clients in order to build relationships with the customers.

"I always enjoyed being outside in the natural environment, and understanding how everything interacted always fascinated me."

~ Chris Pettit

Science

Chris Pettit
Manager

College/University (undergraduate): **Sheffield Hallam University** (Sheffield, UK)
Major: **Environmental Management**
College/University (graduate): **Sheffield Hallam University** (Sheffield, UK)
MBA: **Environmental Management for Business**

Description of your profession:
I perform Environmental Impact Analysis for future development activities. This development includes buildings, trainlines, mining operations and even space stations!

Why did you choose this profession?
I always enjoyed being outside in the natural environment, and understanding how everything interacted always fascinated me.

What is interesting about your profession?
Each project has different impacts to analyze depending on the type of project and its location, from geography, geology, air, water, noise, people, flora and fauna...the list is almost endless.

What do you like most about your profession?
1.   Getting to work on cool projects like building new space stations!
2.   Learning how other environmental impacts relate to each other. Like how rebuilding after Superstorm Sandy has an impact on endangered bird and bat populations in New Jersey.
3.   I work with different people all over the country on projects all over the country.

"I have always been drawn to social service."

~ Deborah Day

Deborah Day
Coalition Manager / Community Activist

College/University (undergraduate): **Georgetown University** (Washington, DC)
Major: **Political Science**
College/University (graduate): **Cornell University** (Ithaca, NY)
MBA: **Master of Business Administration - Concentration in Finance**

Description of your profession:
I help support family caregivers who take care of a loved one who either has a physical or mental disability or issues with aging. My company's mission is to give access to resources and support to those caregivers. We want to help them become better caregivers.

Why did you choose this profession?
I have always been drawn to social service, even while I was involved in a more traditional corporate career.

What is interesting about your profession?
People share their personal stories and struggles and victories with me every day.

What do you like most about your profession?
1. Helping people solve problems.
2. Meeting and working with new and interesting people every day.
3. People call me and email me all the time to say "thank you" for what I do to help them.

"I chose this career because I like to help people with their problems."

~ Craig Oliver

Social Skills

Craig Oliver
Mental Health Therapist

College/University: **Virginia State University** (Petersburg, VA)
Major: **Interdisciplinary Studies (IDST) Family Science**

Description of your profession:
I counsel with emphasis on prevention. I work with individuals and groups to promote optimum mental and emotional health. I may help individuals deal with issues associated with addictions, substance abuse, family, parenting, marriage, stress, self-esteem and aging.

Why did you choose this profession?
I chose this career because I like to help people with their problems.

What is interesting about your profession?
Solving people's problems when they give up, thereby giving them hope.

What do you like most about your profession?
1. I like meeting people.
2. The pay is great!
3. Being a hero to some clients in the community.

"I chose Social Work because I love people and many people need help."

~ Lisette Lombana

Social Work

Lissette Lombana
Student Assistance Counselor / Coach

College/University (undergraduate): Rutgers University School of Social Work (New Brunswick, NJ)
Major: Social Work
College/University (graduate): Rutgers University (New Brunswick, NJ)
MSW: Social Work, Direct Practice
College/University (graduate): Fairleigh Dickinson University (Teaneck, NJ)
MA: Administrative Science, Certificate Community Development
Other education/certification: Licensed School Social Worker, Licensed Student Assistance Counselor

Description of your profession:
I am able to enjoy two professions. As a Student Assistance Counselor, I help people when they are having a difficult time with something. I help them feel better, stronger and happier. As a coach, I teach sports to athletes who want to learn and get better.

Why did you choose this profession?
I chose Social Work because I love people and many people need help. I also love sports and I want to share what I've learned with others.

What is interesting about your profession?
I meet so many great people and get to help them. And with sports, I enjoy the excitement of watching someone accomplish a goal and the thrill of winning.

What do you like most about your profession?
1. Meeting many different people and every day is different.
2. As a Student Assistance Counselor, I can be creative in trying to find a solution.
3. As a Coach, I get to travel all over to play teams and meet great people.

"I LOVE the game of tennis and couldn't think of a better way to live my life than to play tennis every day!"

~ Gentree Van Blake

Sports

Gentree Van Blake
Professional Tennis Instructor

College/University: **Boston University** (Boston, MA)
Major/Minor: **Economics/Fine Arts**
Other education/certification: **United States Tennis Association (USTA) Tennis Professional, United States Professional Tennis Registry (USPTR)**

Description of your profession:
I coach/teach tennis to children and adults from a beginner level all the way up to nationally ranked competitors.

Why did you choose this profession?
After college I had great jobs in investment banking and I earned a decent salary, however, after a few years, I began not to like what I was doing. I decided to take some time off to figure out what I wanted to do. One day I looked over in the corner at my racquet that hadn't gotten much use while I was a Banker. I figured I'd give it a shot...and the rest is history. I LOVE the game of tennis and couldn't think of a better way to live my life than to play tennis every day!

What is interesting about your profession?
The most interesting thing about teaching tennis is having to develop ways that people can learn very complex concepts in a very simple way.

What do you like most about your profession?
1. I love playing tennis so I NEVER have to work...all I do is play!
2. I get to be outdoors during the Spring, Summer and Fall seasons. No office for me!
3. Being able to help tennis players become more confident players and human beings is highly gratifying.

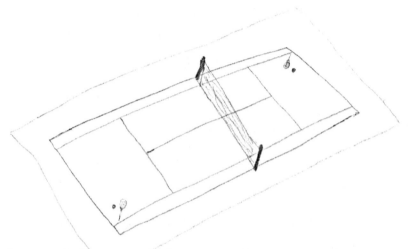

"I learned the game of tennis when I was about 5 years old, and fell in love with it."

~ Steven Capo

Sports

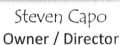

Steven Capo
Owner / Director

College/University: **Rutgers University** (New Brunswick, NJ)
Major/Minor: **Journalism/English**
Other education/certification: **USTA Tennis Professional**

Description of your profession:
My tennis facility provides instructional tennis lessons, tennis team practice and matches, as well as, personalized fitness training.

Why did you choose this profession?
I learned the game of tennis when I was about 5 years old, and fell in love with it. From as far back as I can remember, I always wanted the sport to be a part of my life, either competing or instructing.

What is interesting about your profession?
Watching students develop and achieve goals while simultaneously (at the same time) creating a positive environment around them.

What do you like most about your profession?
1. Getting to wear fitness clothes every day to work.
2. Meeting famous professional tennis players.
3. Getting to playing tennis all of the time.

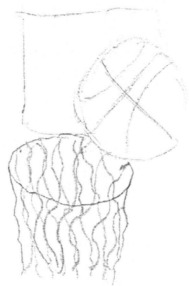

"I've always had the love of basketball, teaching, and making a difference with our youth."

~ William R. Howze

Sports Management

William R. Howze
Men's Basketball Director of Operations

College/University: **University of Maryland – College Park** (College Park, MD)
Major/Minor: **Social Studies/Education**
Other education/certification: **Advanced Professional Certificate – Social Studies**

Description of your profession:

I manage various professional and administrative day-to-day operations for a Men's Basketball NCAA Division 1 Program. A few of my responsibilities include organizing game tickets, uploading games and downloading games of opponent teams, watching film, organizing study hall, checking classes and coordinating community events. I also act as a liaison with all of our coaches and other athletic and administrative staff members.

Why did you choose this profession?

I always had the love of basketball, teaching, and making a difference with our youth. I was the head coach of a high school basketball team and assistant coach at a college university, which gave me the desire to be on the administration side of the business.

What is interesting about your profession?

My profession is interesting because I have the ability to use my coaching skills, education skills and organizational skills in my daily day-to-day operations.

What do you like most about your profession?

1. Coordinating team travel and traveling with the team throughout the United States and internationally as well!
2. Assisting with official and unofficial visits and directing the recruiting process per NCAA policy and procedures.
3. Assisting the Head Coach in scheduling games and overseeing game contracts.

"The profession chose me. I took an interest in designing technology."

~ Shaun Waters

Technology

Shaun Waters
Software Quality Assurance Manager

College/University: **College of Holy Cross** (Worcester, MA)
Major: **English Literature**

Description of your profession:
I manage a team of people who test software to make sure that it works as designed.

Why did you choose this profession?
The profession chose me. I took an interest in designing technology. I also became good at identifying and solving problems with application designs.

What is interesting about your profession?
We get to break computer programs all day. Our job is to make sure that it does not break when you use it.

What do you like most about your profession?
1. Getting to see how a cool app is created after all of the hard work.
2. Having a good team. It is important to work hard, but laugh a little bit when things don't go perfectly.
3. Figuring out why something isn't working right. It feels good when you solve the mystery.

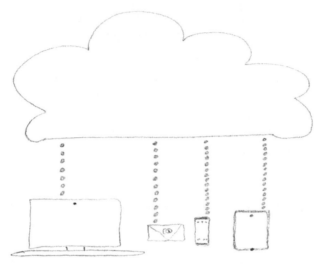

"I really didn't know what I wanted to be, but I was open to new opportunities and took a chance when it came my way."

~ Adriana Zeman

High Tech / Software

Adriana Zeman
Vice President, Customer Success

College/University (undergraduate): **University of California, Santa Cruz** (Santa Cruz, CA)
Major/Minor: **Latin American & Latino Studies**
College/University (graduate): **F.W. Olin Graduate School of Business, Babson College** (Wellesley, MA)
Other education/certification: **Graduate Certificate in Public Relations, Emerson College** (Boston, MA)

Description of your profession:
I started my career as a Project Manager. Today, I run all of the post sales experience for a SaaS (Software as a Service) software startup company. This means that right after a customer signs our contract, they work with people on my team to implement the cloud-based software, learn how to use it, and do more and more over time.

Why did you choose this profession?
By accident really. I am very organized and I like creating and defining processes. I really didn't know what I wanted to be, but I was open to new opportunities and took a chance when it came my way.

What is interesting about your profession?
I get to learn about a lot of different customers and their businesses, and because we are a young company in a very young industry, I get to be really creative and experiment a lot.

What do you like most about your profession?
1. The environment. We are a small company and we're all in one room together collaborating (working together) all the time.
2. I like to learn new things about my customers, technology and our industry.
3. The people I work with make my days fun.

213

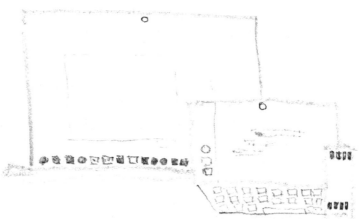

"Every day I get to discover and experiement with new ideas on how to prepare youth to take their rightful place in the future."

~ Kalimah Priforce

Technology

Kalimah Priforce
Headmaster Chief Executive Officer

College/University: **University of Oxford** (3PA, UK) / **CUNY BA** (New York, NY)
Major/Minor: **Global Business Strategy/Urban Youth Studies**

Description of your profession:

As Headmaster of an inclusive innovation company, I prepare youth and their mentors to build web and mobile apps that accelerate college and career pathways in STEAM (Science, Technology, Engineering, Art Design, and Mathematics).

Why did you choose this profession?

I started my first computer tech company at the age of 16 and sold it at 19. After my younger brother was shot and killed behind our childhood elementary school, I committed my love for education, technology and business, into eliminating barriers to a child's greatest potential.

What is interesting about your profession?

Every day I get to discover and experiment with new ideas on how to prepare youth to take their rightful place in the future. So I think about the future a lot, and how to design a better future for the work, beginning with low opportunity youth.

What do you like most about your profession?

1. I get to manage an incredible team who are dedicated to transforming children's lives.
2. Finding ways to create middle ground between public and private interests and create business models that lead to sustainable impact and change.
3. The kids whose lives I make a difference, are an extension of the love I have for my brother, and the thousands of kids I came across as a group home orphan in Brooklyn.

215

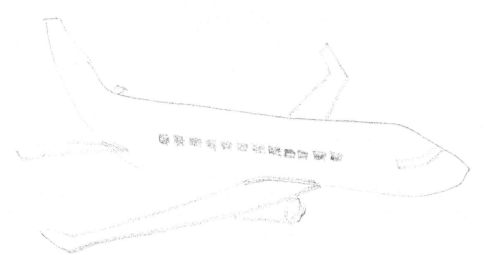

"After learning a great deal about owning and operating a business, I decided to start my own."

~ Ann Evans-Bacile

Travel / Fitness

Ann Evans-Bacile
Owner / President / Group Fitness Trainer

College/University: **Travel & Tourism Institute** (Sacramento, CA) / **Cittone College** (Ramsey, NJ)
Major/Minor: **Corporate Travel/Meeting Event Planning**

Description of your profession:
I own a travel company. I have pharmaceutical company clients for whom I plan and book travel arrangements, and coordinate regional and international meetings, ensuring their corporate business trips run smoothly. I am also a Group Fitness Trainer, and in this profession I implement training programs in both large and small group fitness settings.

Why did you choose this profession?
I started a travel company at the age of 23 with a business partner. I learned a great deal about owning and operating a business, and after 8 years, I decided to start my own company. I work within one of the largest privately held travel agencies in the United States. I do this to utilize the advantages of working with a large company while still managing my own clients. While working at my corporate job, I saw people struggle with weight loss and the adverse effects of diet medications, and as a result, I began to get into fitness.

What is interesting about your profession?
Working with a wide variety of people with varied interests and backgrounds.

What do you like most about your profession?
1. Working with medical professionals all of the world and facing all of the challenges that come from working in an ever changing industry.
2. Creating a fun and inviting environment.
3. Sharing my love of exercise with amazing people and helping them reach their fitness goals.

217

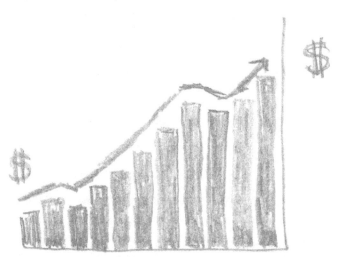

"I've been involved in sports my entire life and I'm a competitive person, therefore, the Sales and Marketing field was a great fit."

~ Kyle Anglin

Wholesale Management

Kyle Anglin
National Sales Director

College/University: **Saint Bonaventure University** (Saint Bonaventure, NY)
Major: **Sociology**

Description of your profession:
I am an athletic footwear executive, directly responsible for managing 7 Account Managers nationally, account implementation, increasing sales, managing financials, consulting and vendor relations. I work with and manage Account Managers across the country, and oversee and monitor the manner in which they service our brand. Our primary goal is to increase sales every year while maintaining, strengthening, and establishing the brand in the market place.

Why did you choose this profession?
I've been involved in sports my entire life and I'm a competitive person, therefore, the Sales and Marketing field was a great fit.

What is interesting about your profession?
What makes what I do interesting is that I'm faced with new challenges daily. A major challenge in the athletic/fashion footwear industry is staying relevant and cool to the core consumer. We do this buy soliciting information from potential customers, working with new and up-and-coming entertainers, and also working with really cool athletes.

What do you like most about your profession?
1. Traveling globally (Canada, Europe)
2. Meeting new and interesting people daily.
3. I have a direct influence on fashion trends in the United States.

219

"My work is NEVER boring and never feels like a job."
~ Ingrid Marcroft

Yoga & Spirituality

Ingrid A. Marcroft
Co-Owner / Yoga Instructor / Interfaith Minister

College/University: **Houghton College (Houghton, NY) and La Sorbonne** (Paris, France)
Major/Minor: **French/Philosophy and Vocal Performance**

Description of your profession:
I own and manage a neighborhood yoga studio in New York City with my husband. I teach yoga to all kinds of people, and I am also an Interfaith Minister, which means that I create and perform ceremonies (such as weddings) and help people get along with each other.

Why did you choose this profession?
I spent many years trying to figure out how to be of service in the world. Finally, figuring out how to feel connected to my body and my spirit made me so happy, that I wanted to share what I learned.

What is interesting about your profession?
The yoga world (and business) is constantly expanding. It allows me to be completely myself as I teach and pass on this ancient art of self-care and self-development, all over the world, in my own unique way.

What do you like most about your profession?
1.   Meeting such awesome people every day and making them smile by inspiring them to be the best possible people they can be spiritually, emotionally, mentally, and physically. We all get to play together and stay healthy!
2.   My work is NEVER boring and never feels like a job.
3.   My husband and I have created a home for a wonderful and loving community of people whom we love and respect and who love and respect us.

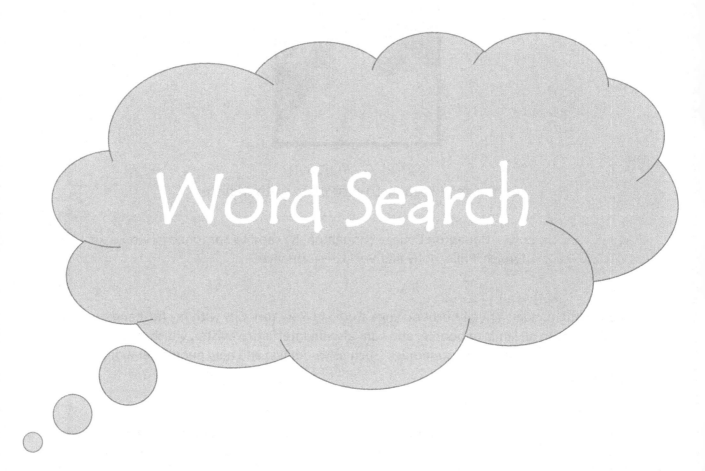

Word Search

When I Grow Up...
Just Imagine.™

```
G  R  K  J  D  P  L  G  B  C  S  D  W  A  R  V  O
N  C  P  I  R  W  V  P  R  O  F  E  S  S  I  O  N
C  L  Q  A  T  T  J  X  I  M  P  A  E  Z  D  L  T
M  Y  M  Y  S  N  K  I  S  V  H  S  I  V  P  U  H
L  E  R  C  Y  S  B  Y  P  Z  P  L  N  B  C  N  G
E  N  N  Y  I  F  I  M  A  G  I  N  E  T  J  T  A
Q  C  L  T  B  N  D  O  N  E  T  W  O  R  K  E  P
X  O  K  P  O  N  E  J  N  E  R  M  A  X  A  E  E
B  U  A  F  P  R  A  H  K  X  W  Z  Y  T  Y  R  X
E  R  P  L  C  J  S  A  M  P  S  H  A  D  O  W  C
H  A  T  P  L  A  Y  P  W  L  R  W  P  P  R  L  I
P  G  R  A  D  E  S  P  P  O  L  S  T  U  D  Y  T
Y  E  A  L  H  Z  A  Y  O  R  E  A  D  R  G  L  E
L  D  U  T  W  I  A  D  S  E  A  I  E  S  O  P  M
O  P  V  I  S  U  A  L  I  Z  E  C  G  U  A  O  E
O  I  U  B  L  L  M  O  T  I  V  A  T  E  L  R  N
Q  G  D  O  P  B  H  W  I  Z  S  P  D  I  S  P  T
P  V  O  B  I  H  T  S  V  C  H  Z  E  S  C  I  R
I  N  D  U  S  T  R  Y  E  Y  L  F  G  W  S  E  G
```

Search for the following words:

Encourage	Happy	Motivate	Practice	Visualize
Excitement	Ideas	Network	Profession	Volunteer
Explore	Imagine	Passion	Read	
Goals	Lead	Play	Shadow	
Grades	Mentor	Positive	Study	

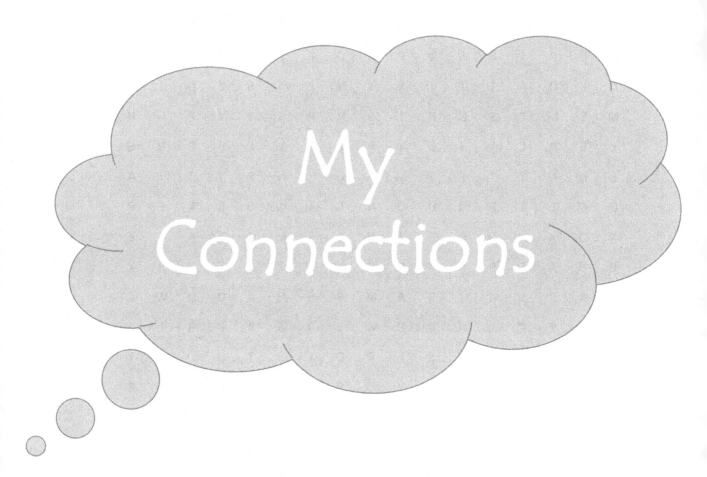

My Connections

In the My Connections section, there are blank **profession templates**. You can interview someone in a profession that you are interested in learning more about. Don't forget to add their picture!

Try starting with your parents. I'm sure you will learn something new about what they do!

Profession/Industry:

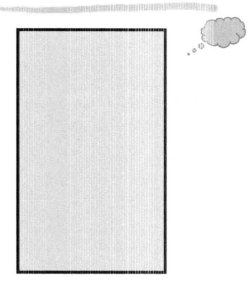

Name: _____

Title: _____

College/University: _____

Major: _____

Description of your profession:

_____

_____

Why did you choose this profession?

_____

What is interesting about your profession?

_____

What do you like most about your profession?

1. _____

2. _____

3. _____

Profession/Industry:

Name: _____

Title: _____

College/University: _____

Major: _____

Description of your profession:

_____

_____

Why did you choose this profession?

_____

What is interesting about your profession?

_____

What do you like most about your profession?

1. _____

2. _____

3. _____

Profession/Industry:

Name: _____

Title: _____

College/University: _____

Major: _____

Description of your profession:

_____

_____

Why did you choose this profession?

_____

What is interesting about your profession?

_____

What do you like most about your profession?

1. _____

2. _____

3. _____

Profession/Industry:

Name: _____

Title: _____

College/University: _____

Major: _____

Description of your profession:

_____

_____

Why did you choose this profession?

_____

What is interesting about your profession?

_____

What do you like most about your profession?

1. _____

2. _____

3. _____

Profession/Industry:

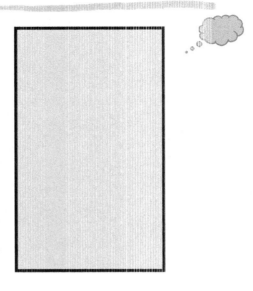

Name: _____

Title: _____

College/University: _____

Major: _____

Description of your profession:

_____

_____

Why did you choose this profession?

_____

What is interesting about your profession?

_____

What do you like most about your profession?

1. _____

2. _____

3. _____

Profession/Industry:

Name: _____

Title: _____

College/University: _____

Major: _____

Description of your profession:

_____

_____

Why did you choose this profession?

_____

What is interesting about your profession?

_____

What do you like most about your profession?

1. _____

2. _____

3. _____

Profession/Industry:

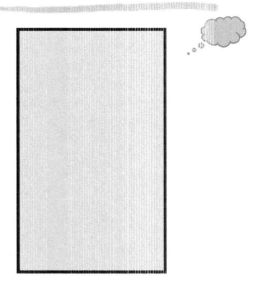

Name: _____

Title: _____

College/University: _____

Major: _____

Description of your profession:

_____

_____

Why did you choose this profession?

_____

What is interesting about your profession?

_____

What do you like most about your profession?

1. _____

2. _____

3. _____

Profession/Industry:

Name: _____

Title: _____

College/University: _____

Major: _____

Description of your profession:

_____

_____

Why did you choose this profession?

_____

What is interesting about your profession?

_____

What do you like most about your profession?

1. _____

2. _____

3. _____

Profession/Industry:

Name: _____

Title: _____

College/University: _____

Major: _____

Description of your profession:

_____

_____

Why did you choose this profession?

_____

What is interesting about your profession?

_____

What do you like most about your profession?

1. _____

2. _____

3. _____

Profession/Industry:

Name: _____

Title: _____

College/University: _____

Major: _____

Description of your profession:

_____

_____

Why did you choose this profession?

_____

What is interesting about your profession?

_____

What do you like most about your profession?

1. _____

2. _____

3. _____

List of
Professions

List of Professions*

When I Grow Up...
Just Imagine.™

Accountant
Activist
Actor/Actress
Actuary
Acupuncturist
Adjuster
Administrator
Advertiser
Advertising
Aerospace Engineer
Agent
Agricultural Technician
Agriculturist
Air Traffic Controller
Aircraft Mechanic
Allergist
Anchor Man/Woman
Animal Trainer
Animator
Anthropologist
Appraiser
Archeologist
Architect
Art Director
Artist
Appraiser
Assessor
Astrologer
Astronaut
Astronomer
Athlete
Athletic Trainer
Atmospheric and Space Scientist
Attorney
Audio and Video Equipment Technician
Audiologist

Auditor
Author
Auto Electrician
Aviation Inspector
Baker
Banker
Barber
Beautician
Beekeeper
Biochemist
Biologist
Biotechnologist
Bookkeeper
Botanist
Broadcaster
Builder
Building Inspector
Business Man/Woman
Butcher
Buyer
Camera Operator
Captain
Cardiologist
Carpenter
Cartoonist
Chaplain
Chef
Chemical Engineer
Chemist
Chiropractor
Choreographer
Civil Engineer
Civil Service Clerk
Claim Adjuster
Clergy
Clinical Data Manager

List of Professions*

When I Grow Up...
Just Imagine.™

Coach
Columnist
Comedian
Commentator
Communications
Community Service
Community Specialist
Compliance Management
Composer
Computer and Information Research Science
Computer and Information Systems
Computer Hardware Engineer
Computer Network Architect
Computer Operations
Computer Programming
Computer Software Engineer
Computer System Analyst
Conductor
Construction
Construction Engineer
Construction Management
Controller
Cook
Copy Writer
Coroner
Correction Officer
Cosmetologist
Counselor
Creative Director
Credit Analyst
Curator
Custodian
Customer Service
Customs Inspection
Dancer
Data Communications Analyst

Database Administration
Dean of Students
Decorator
Dentist
Deputy
Dermatologist
Designer
Detective and Criminal Investigation
Developer
Dietician
Disc Jockey
Doctor
Ecologist
Economist
Editor
Education Administrator
Educator
Electrical Drafter
Electrical Engineer
Electrician
Emergency Management
Engineer
Entrepreneur
Environmental Restoration
Environmental Science
Ergonomist
Farmer
Fashion Designer
Film and Video Production
Filmmaker
Finance
Financial Adviser
Financial Analyst
Fire Fighter
Fire Inspector
Fire Marshall

List of Professions*

Fire Safety
Fisherman
Flight Attendant
Flight Engineer
Florist
Gardener
Geneticist
Geographer
Geologist
Geophysicist
Government Service
Governor
Graphic Artist
Graphic Designer
Hacker
Hair Stylist
Historian
Human Resources
Illustrator
Industrial Engineer
Information Security Analyst
Information Technology
Inspector
Instructor
Insurance Adjuster
Insurance Underwriter
Interior Designer
Interpreter and Translator
Investment Banker
Investment Broker
Investment Fund Management
Jeweler
Journalist
Judge
Judicial Law Clerk
Labor Relations

Landscape Architect
Lawyer
Lecturer
Legislator
Librarian
Linguist
Loan Officer
Lobbyist
Logistics Analyst
Logistics Engineer
Loss Prevention
Machinist
Mail Carrier
Maintenance and Repair
Manufacturer
Martial Artist
Marine Architect
Marine Biologist
Marine Engineer
Market Research
Marketer
Marketing
Marshal
Mason
Mathematician
Mayor
Mechanic
Mechanical Engineering Designer
Media
Medical Biller
Medical and Health Services
Merchandising
Merchant
Meteorologist
Military Officer
Minister

List of Professions*

Model	Playwright
Mortgage Broker	Plumber
Multimedia Designer	Podiatrist
Musician	Police Detective
Network Systems Analyst	Police Officer
Neurologist	Political Scientist
Newscaster	Politician
Nuclear Engineer	Postal Worker
Nurse	President
Nurse Practioner	Priest
Nutritionist	Principal
Obstetrician	Private Detective
Occupational Therapy	Producer
Ophthalmologist	Production Management
Optician	Professor
Optometrist	Programmer
Orthodontist	Project Management
Orthopedist	Proofreader
Painter	Psychiatrist
Paleontologist	Psychologist
Paralegal	Psychotherapist
Paramedic	Public Administration
Pastor	Public Relations
Patent Agent	Public Speaker
Patent Attorney	Publisher
Pediatrician	Quality Assurance
Periodontist	Quality Control
Pharmaceuticals	Quality Inspector
Pharmacist	Rabbi
Philanthropist	Radio and TV
Philosopher	Radio Personality
Photographer	Radiologist
Physical Therapist	Railway Engine Mechanic
Physician	Real Estate Broker
Physicist	Real Estate Developer
Pilot	Receptionist

List of Professions*

When I Grow Up...
Just Imagine.™

Record Producer
Recreational Therapist
Recycling Management
Referee
Registered Nurse
Registrar
Researcher
Respiratory Therapist
Road Transport Technician
Safety Engineer
Safety Inspector
Sales Man/Woman
Scientist
Screenwriter
Secretary
Securities, Commodities and Financial Services
Security
Senator
Sergeant-At-Arms
Service Mechanic
Singer
Social and Community Service
Social Worker
Sociologist
Software Engineer
Soldier
Songwriter
Sound Engineer
Speech Therapist
Sports Agent
Sports Medicine Physician
Statistician
Stock Broker

Superintendent
Supervisor
Surgeon
Surveyor
Systems Analyst
Systems Engineer
Tax Consultant
Teacher
Technical Support
Technician
Telecommunications
Textile Technologist
Therapist
Translator
Travel Agent
Treasurer
Tutor
Undertaker
Underwriter
Utility Worker
Vendor
Veterinarian
Video Game Developer
Videographer
Waste Management
Web Designer
Web Developer
Welder
Writer
Zookeeper
Zoologist

*This is not a complete list of professions.
Please note: Within each profession there may be many types of jobs and job titles (i.e., Assistant, Coordinator, Manager, Director, Vice President, President, Chief Executive, etc.).

Thought Bubble Tips

Thought Bubble Tips

Refer to the Thought Bubble Tips regularly.

1. Imagine

2. Passion

3. Visualize

4. Goals

5. Read

6. Grades

7. Practice

8. Encourage

9. Lead

10. Mentor

11. Shadow

12. Volunteer

13. Network

14. Happy

Thought Bubble Tips are on pages 9 – 37.

Thought Bubble Tips

#1 Advocate

Parents & Guardians

Dear Parents and Guardians:

You are your child's **#1 advocate**. Continue to encourage them to imagine, tune-in to their passions, read, set goals, take the lead, join groups and team activities, get the best grades and think positively. Be creative, there are many ways to guide and encourage them...

- **Discover** – Help your child discover their passions. Pay close attention to the things they like to do the most.

- **Develop** – You may notice your child's talents and your child may not realize it or even show an interest. Guide them (without pressure) and try to develop their talents. It may turn out to be something they really enjoy.

- **Motivate** – Whatever your child's interest, try to nurture it. Think of ways to give them more exposure to it. Consider having your child attend enrichment classes and/or specialty summer camps. Also, consider connecting with people in that area of interest.

- **Inspire** – If your child shows interest in a profession, put up a photo or poster with images of that profession in their room. Let them know that their dreams are attainable and let them visualize it.

- **Shadow** – Think about letting a child shadow you. You can arrange with a friend to take each other's child to work so that they can experience each other's parents profession.

- **Mentor** – Consider mentoring a child. It's fulfilling!

Please remind your child to revisit the **thought bubble** tips. These are steps that they can look back on in the years to come. Time goes by rather quickly. Take the time to explore the possibilities with your children and remember *When I Grow Up...Just Imagine.*

Respectfully Yours,
Erica Brown Oliver

Pursue

Parents/Guardians:
What about you?

Dear Parents and Guardians:

Do you have dreams that you haven't fulfilled? Well, it is not too late. Take some time for yourself. YOU shouldn't get lost in the sauce! Yes, you are busy with your own job, taking the children to activities, programs, events, and continually juggling the day to day. However, you shouldn't let your own dreams fade away or let your talents get dusty. Make some time for you.

Are there things that you wish you could have accomplished? Is there something that you have always wanted to do or try, however, never made the time for it? Was there something that you loved to do, but gave it up because life got in the way? Well, guess what? It is not too late. It is okay to seek out new or old interest, at any age. Go for it now! You don't want to look back and say, "I should have tried to ..." Time flies and it is better to say that you did try versus you should have tried. Whether it is learning a new skillset, starting your own business, learning a new language or learning how to swim. Whatever it is, start off small. Ease in to it. Make a vision board, set goals and pursue!

I know it is hard to carve out the time for yourself, but it is important. Taking the time out to do what you love to do, will be fulfilling and gratifying, and that happiness will also exude on to your children. And, who wouldn't want that?

Start now! It is not too late...

...Just imagine.

Respectfully Yours,
Erica Brown Oliver

Conclusion

My hope is that this book shows you that you can be anything that you want to be when you grow up. And, as I mentioned in the beginning, it is okay if you do not know right now. My dream is that you find what you love to do and you pursue it.

I would love for you to keep this book as a resource and continue to flip through the professions and the thought bubble tips. And remember, this is just a glimpse of some of the many professions that are out there. There are so many more! Endless possibilities...

...Just Imagine.

The Author's Inspiration...

This book has been a passion project for Erica Brown Oliver.

Watching her children, as early as 5 years old, get asked the question "What do you want to be when you grow up?", made her flash back to her own childhood, and being asked the very same question at such a young age. This is when the book idea came to her. She wanted to let children know that they shouldn't feel the pressure in elementary nor middle school, as they haven't even been exposed to the vast amount of professions out there yet.

Her idea was to give children exposure to as many professions early on, so that they could be aware of how many careers there are. She wanted to inspire children to tune-in to their passions, and if they found something they were passionate about, to take steps to pursue it. As she believes, if you love what you do for a living, it doesn't feel like work.

She reached out to her friends near and far, to ask them if they would be willing to share their professions with young readers, and with their overwhelmingly positive response, her interviews began. Each person featured was more than happy to participate! There were so many kind words and well wishes. Many expressed that they wished there was a book like this when they were growing up, and they couldn't wait to share it with their own children.

Erica encourages her children to explore their passions and to think...
When I Grow Up...Just Imagine.

Acknowledgements

I would like to thank my amazing, wonderful husband, David Patrick Oliver, for his love and support. (Especially through all of the late nights tapping on my laptop). I would like to thank my beautiful, smart and talented children, both of whom contributed to *When I Grow Up...Just Imagine*. – Madison Michelle Oliver, as Editor and Brendan David Oliver as Illustrator. I am so proud of you!!!

I would like to thank each and every friend who participated in this book project. Each friend that I reached out to, replied with overwhelming words of praise for the project. And many reiterating that they themselves did not know what they wanted to be and how helpful they thought this book would be for their own children.

I would like to thank – My mom, Ethele Harvin Brown, for her unconditional love, support and wisdom; who always encourages me to go for it. My dad, Elmo Ronald Brown, who I miss deeply; I know he is saying "I am so proud of you sweetheart." My fabulous sister, Elaine Meryl Brown, for always saying I'm doing a great job. You are too!
And, my dearest friends, who expressed immediate excitement and sent good vibes my way through this whole process; Sharon "Wink" Daniels, Audrey De Shong, Maxine Gooden, Candace Green, Candice Hardiman and Monique Moore Pryor. Thank you.

Made in the USA
Las Vegas, NV
28 April 2021

22144171R00149